Bottled Walla

Sam McLeod

Best,
SAM

To My Girls
Much Love,
Dad

The Beginning

Hi. My name is Sam. Well, it's not really Sam. As I explained in my first book called *Welcome to Walla Walla,* Sam is my pen name—mostly because I just like the name Sam. I don't have anything to hide but the pen name makes people think I do. I've found this makes me a more interesting person.

Believe it or not, there were enough folks who liked my first book that I felt like I could make some sense out of writing another one. People who read the book would stop me on the street and say things like, "For a first book, it wasn't so bad," or "Hey, I really liked the picture on the cover of your book." I took that as encouragement.

I don't mean to say that there wasn't criticism of the first book. Goodness knows there was plenty of it. It turns out that I made so many mistakes and have so many faults that, as folks pointed them out to me, I had to write them down because I couldn't remember them all. What I learned from all the negative energy was that folks want me to quit murdering the English language and get my grammar right. Well, as unnatural as that is for me, I'm working on it; so please let me know if you think I improve my command of the written word this time around.

After I finished writing the first book I went off to find out how to get it printed and into stores where people could buy it. There was a lot to learn about editing, formatting, cover design, finding a printer, copyright laws, the Library of Congress book cataloguing system, and on and on. I'm glad I learned so much, but mostly because I'll know what to avoid this time around. The main thing I learned from the process is that I like writing and meeting the people who read my writing, but not much else about book publishing.

Annie, my wife and best friend, is the psychoanalyst in our family. She is pretty sure that she owns 100% of our combined emotional intelligence. She thinks my love of writing stems from a basic hermit-like preference for solitude, a tendency toward pathological lying, and early childhood issues with control. She might be right. I don't pretend to know. I will admit that I like hiding out, making up stories to tell, and having the characters in a book do what I tell them to do.

Now, you'll notice that I just introduced Annie as my best friend, which she is. I learned from the last book that saying a nice thing about Annie on the printed page where other people can see it does wonders for Annie's good humor. It turns out that her good humor is a good thing for both of us.

I also learned from writing the last book that folks expect writers to be a bit on the eccentric end of the bell curve, which means that you get away with stuff that folks used to call you on. I really like this part of being a writer. This alone is reason enough to continue my writing career.

Okay, enough for now about my book writing and what I've learned. Let's move on to this book. Since Annie and I moved over here to Walla Walla from Seattle, our friends and family have been asking us, "Why Walla Walla?"

When we get this question, we tend to wax eloquent about all of Walla Walla's great qualities . . . and there are plenty. When you boil it all down though, the simple answer is that we like the way of life over here. Life here is slower, quieter, and closer to the earth. It's a place where other people have time for you, and you for them. It's a place where you can do something different in your life. So, in many ways, this book is not so much about Walla Walla as it is about finding quieter places where folks can follow their dreams.

In the first book, I invited interesting folks to get in touch with me and tell me why they're interesting so I'd have some good stories to write about them and put in this book. It will not surprise you that a bunch of people called me up; we had coffee or a drink (sometimes more than one); I heard their stories; and I found that a few of them actually were interesting— not generally as interesting as they thought, but interesting enough to write a story about.

In this book there are stories about some of the people around here who are pursuing their dreams, stories about our own dream chasing, stories about being part of a small rural community, stories about becoming a writer, and stories about everyday living out here on the prairie. Maybe these stories will help answer the "Why Walla Walla?" question. I hope so.

Now, before I launch into the stories, I have to say again that I freely admit a tendency to lose track of facts from time to time. Most folks call it "artistic license." Annie calls it lying. Well, maybe it is. Anyway, I hope you're not one of those people who believe everything they read.

And just one more thing—like I said in the first book, I was born and bred in Nashville, Tennessee. I've never gotten over it. I talk "slow" so I'm recommending that you read this book "slow." If you do, at least there's a chance it'll make some sense to you. I hope so.

Anyway, here goes . . .

Best,
SAM

Update

Note to Readers: You will see in this letter that I'm starting to use some big words like "ostensibly" and "compunction" in an effort to expand my vocabulary. I hope you are paying attention and giving me some credit for the considerable effort I'm putting in.

Dear George:

You have a good memory. I'm impressed. It was just about a year ago that we bought some land here in Walla Walla and started on our new lives as farmers. It has been a good ride so far. Some folks would laugh at our use of the word "farmers" but that's how we choose to describe ourselves—sort of an if-you-believe-it-it'll-come-true way of viewing our place in the food chain. You asked about the farm, the new house, the kids, Walla Walla, and what else we are doing around here. Well, that is a lot to report on in one letter but I'll give it a shot.

What we used to (and still sometimes do) call "The Land" is now called Detour Farm, ostensibly because it's located on Detour Road but also because it pretty well describes what we've done in our lives recently—detouring off the predictable path to explore another small corner of the world. As you may remember, The Land is roughly 160 acres of former cattle pasture that we are slowly converting into a small preserve for wildlife. We've moved the cattle off of the farm, and have started planting drought resistant grasses and shrubs that will provide cover, water and food for quail, pheasant, ducks, geese, hawks, heron, deer and a big group of wild turkeys that have recently taken up residence along the Walla Walla River at our back door.

Just about every night as the last bit of sunlight turns to dark, Annie and I sit out on the front porch and watch the turkeys peck their way along the ridge just below the house before they move to their roosts in the trees along the river. It is so quiet and still out here that we can hear the frogs croaking along the riverbank and coyotes howling in the distance. We were looking for solitude and I reckon we've found it.

Greg, our builder, finished the house back in January and we moved right in. The barn and small cottage have just been completed so we're very close to being settled. There are still a bunch of boxes to sort through someday, but they're all stuffed into the barn and our old Airstream trailer, and are far enough from view that neither of us feels any compunction to hurry out there and finish the job of unpacking. We seem to have found everything we need; so goodness knows what's in those unopened boxes anyway.

We love our new place—particularly the barn-like feel of the house, the basalt stone fireplace and the covered porch that faces the Blue Mountains to the east of us. I've managed to log a lot of hours on that porch already—mostly just watching the scenery play out and the stars move by overhead. We only get about eight inches of rain a year, so there are plenty of bright sunny days and clear cool nights—quite a big change from misty Seattle.

We can just begin to see fledgling blades of new grass poking up through the ground around the house. After all the construction, we're working hard to covert our "yard" from what looks like a desert into something that more closely mimics the tall grasses beginning to grow up on the rest of the property. Thank goodness Annie is good at growing greenery. She spends endless hours reading up on plants that'll grow around here and talking to the neighbors about windbreaks and such. All I have to do is dig the occasional hole wherever she says, and move the sprinkler around.

Our girls are thriving. Summer is in Honduras teaching English to grammar school kids who are teaching her Spanish. She says her kids love to sing so she's taught them a bunch of songs in English like "Rocky Top" and "Sittin' on the Dock of the Bay" and "Don't Go Breaking My Heart." I'd love to hear those kids singing these songs in their Spanish accents.

Summer lives in a very small village with a family much like our own—parents who work and three girls ages 6, 8 and 11. Summer says the girls are always trying to take care of her because she doesn't speak Spanish very well and therefore must not be smart enough to take care of herself.

Jolie is finishing up at Whitman College here in Walla Walla. She'll graduate in May. I think she'll miss Whitman and all her friends but she's also ready to test her independence in the outside world. She's going to take a post-graduation trip to New Zealand and Australia to visit friends who are studying there and will tour around with her.

I'm guessing that she'll go on to graduate school in New York in the fall. She'd like to get a graduate degree in early childhood education and then start her own nursery school one of these days. She's always wanted to run her own school and I certainly wouldn't bet against her.

Marshall is about to complete her first year at Central Washington University over in Ellensburg, Washington. You may remember that she was interested in working with chimps in their program where they teach the chimps sign language and talk to them. I'll never forget the day that Marshall told me she wanted to learn to talk to animals—she was just four years old then—and here she is now talking with chimps every day. Amazing, isn't it? Marshall is one of the happiest young ladies on the planet. She loves school, the chimps, and her newfound friends. We couldn't be happier for her.

You wanted to know about Walla Walla and what we're doing over here. In short, Annie is devoting most of her time to raising, training, and showing her alpacas. She's also added a couple of goats to the menagerie. Like Marshall, she's discovering her love for animals and is constantly working with them or talking to newfound friends who share her animal world. She is now talking about shearing her alpacas, spinning their fleece into yarn and weaving blankets. They shear in May, so I guess we'll see how this blanket idea plays out. Maybe someday you'll be the proud owner of a Detour Farm alpaca blanket.

Last weekend, Annie trekked to Portland for a big alpaca show where her youngest cria (baby alpaca) won the "best in show" blue ribbon. She's still grinning about her victory but trying to be modest about it by claiming beginner's luck. We keep pinching ourselves; it's hard to believe that a year ago neither of us knew what an alpaca was and now we own several of them and they're the foundation of Annie's new life.

I spend most of my time writing or working on our land. The writing I can manage; Mother Nature I cannot. So, at least there's some semblance of balance in my life. Exercise takes the form of toting hay bales, tearing out old fence lines, planting trees and shrubs along the riverbank, and building a root cellar. There is no shortage of projects on my "to do" list and that's a good thing.

Walla Walla is a very friendly place; it's been easy to meet folks and begin to blend into the community. We were a little afraid that we'd run out of things to keep us engaged, but so far haven't been able to keep up with all the activities going on around here.

Annie and I are starting a class today on local conservation issues, offered through Walla Walla Community College. Every few months we get a flier from the college telling us about ten to fifteen new courses being offered for seniors (50+). We're often the youngest folks in the class—the ladies referring to me as "young man" and Annie as "that cute young wife of yours." These classes are perfect for us and we're enjoying being the kids again.

On Wednesday nights we often go to Vintage Cellars, a local wine bar, where they show off a local winery and sometimes have live music. On Friday and Saturday nights, we either have a few folks out to the farm or go into town to somebody's house for dinner. This town is full of art galleries, wineries, eateries, live music, and other assorted diversions. It seems like there's a parade, or fair, or farmers' market, or some other community event every weekend. So, there's more than plenty to do.

Anyway, enough about us. Sorry to rattle on. I'm guessing you'll think twice before you ask for another update. So, now it's your turn; please write and let us know what you guys are up to. Annie says to say "hi" to Michelle.

Best,
SAM

Chicago . . . Here We Come

Dear Oprah:

I am writing you again because I am guessing that my first letter to you must have gotten lost in the mail. In it, I was telling you about the book I wrote called *Welcome to Walla Walla* that some folks around here thought might be a good addition to your book club. They were telling me that you have a TV show and that I should watch it to see what it's like and to find out how to get my book in your book club.

So, I did. I watched one of your shows last week and it was pretty good. Now folks around here are telling me that my book is pretty good, too. So maybe there's a good match to be made.

Anyway, I'm writing again to offer to come on your show so you can ask me questions about my book and what it's like being an unknown author. I know your fans would enjoy hearing us chat about such matters. Maybe this would help your ratings and help me sell some books.

I am assuming that you have a pretty good-sized audience; any information you could share with me on this would help me convince Annie, my wife, that taking the time to travel all the way to Chicago would be worthwhile. She thinks I'm just trying to get out of helping her around the farm.

Yesterday, I went with my friend Floyd to the Oasis Restaurant and Bar for breakfast. The Oasis is out near our new house and is a ramshackle old place just full of local color and Floyd's old buddies (at least the ones that are still with us). If you've read my book, you'll know that Floyd and his wife, Mary, were our neighbors while we were renting a place in Walla Walla, waiting for our new house to get built out in the country.

Floyd is 91 years old. He has a little trouble getting around because of a bad hip and uses a cane to walk, but he is doing great otherwise. He doesn't drive any more and Mary doesn't like sitting at a bar in a dive like the Oasis, so every week or two I pick up Floyd and we head on out Stateline Road and settle in on a stool at the Oasis bar where the gang is gathered and usually watching "The Price is Right" on the TV above the bar.

Since Floyd and The Oasis figured so prominently in my book, his buddies are always on Floyd about when he is going to go looking for an agent to handle his movie offers—the ones that'll be coming his way any day now. They razz him about being a celebrity, but I think he enjoys all the attention.

I told the folks at the bar that I'd written to you about coming on your show and that got everybody thinking that Floyd should come along with me so you could talk to the author and one of the real life characters from the book. Cowboy Bob thinks that'd be a double whammy and a sure-fire way to get the entire Oasis bar crowd to watch your show that day. So I asked Floyd if he'd like to go to Chicago and be on "Oprah" with me.

Now to be completely truthful, he didn't know what "Oprah" was so we had to tell him all about your show. Turns out that several of the Oasis regulars are fans of yours. They gave Floyd an earful about sitting in a comfortable chair next to you on a TV stage in front of a bunch of rowdy folks clapping for everything he'd say, and chatting with you—star to star, so to speak. But Floyd said, much to everybody's surprise, that he doesn't really care to be on TV.

I said, "Come on Floyd. It'll be fun. We'll get a trip to Chicago. We'll stay in a fancy hotel and eat fancy meals in the big city for a couple of days. And Oprah will pay for all of it." (I'm assuming that you'd pay for us to come there since it's bound to be cheaper for us to travel to Chicago than for you to travel with a big film crew out here to Walla Walla.)

Well, Floyd wasn't budging. He said he didn't want to be on TV even if we got a free trip . . . that is until his eyes opened up wide and he got a grin on his face and he said, "I've changed my mind. I will go to Chicago and be on TV if we can take the train. I love to ride the train."

So everybody started whooping and hollering because they were going to be seeing both of us together on your show and Cowboy Bob was telling Frank and Nita that he was sure Floyd and I would

15

wave to them from your studio on TV while they were all sitting at the bar at The Oasis watching us.

That's when I threw up my hands and said, "Whoa up a minute. I haven't heard back from Oprah yet, so I don't know whether we're going or when."

Well, that was just like throwing gas on the fire. They all hooted me down saying that I was a real author now and should start having more confidence; plus if Floyd would go, it'd be sure thing.

So, I guess that leaves the question to you. We would be willing to come to Chicago and be on your show and say interesting things, if you will pay for it all.

Now, I'm guessing you'll say yes. So, I took the liberty of calling Floyd this morning and asked him to check his calendar. He says he is free most any day next week but would like a few days notice because he'd like to get a new pair of pants if he's going to be on TV—so he'll look nice. He thinks Mary can take him down to Walla Walla Clothing on Saturday, but, if she's busy, they might not be able to go until Monday. I am also free any day next week. So we could come to Chicago as early as Tuesday if you're anxious to get on with it. I also asked Floyd to check the week after next on the off chance that next week wouldn't work for you, and luckily we are both free everyday that week. So, please let us know what you think.

By the way, on the day I watched your show, you gave everybody in the audience a free gift. If you'd like, I could autograph some of my books and bring them along so you could give one to each of your fans there. They cost $12.95, but I can probably cut 50 cents off the price if you buy enough for the whole crowd.

Best,
SAM

P.S.—Annie, my wife, is now saying that she'd like to come with us. She was snooping around on my desk and found this letter and says that she doesn't think an "Oprah" show with just Floyd and me on it would be as interesting as one that had her alongside us so she could make sure that we don't overstate the truth— which she thinks I have a tendency to do. She also thinks the women who watch your show will want to see what kind of woman it takes to live with a character like me (and I don't think she is using the word "character" as a form of flattery).

She says she wasn't snooping—that the letter was in plain view and begging for her attention. I say bad habits die hard.

At first, she thought this idea of coming to be on your show was ridiculous. So I thought she wasn't interested. She said that Floyd and I could dream all we wanted about being on "Oprah" but it wasn't going to happen. Now she is thinking that stranger things have happened and she doesn't want to be left here in Walla Walla if we get lucky. She says it is okay to change her mind about important things like being on "Oprah."

She could stay in the hotel room with me and she eats like a bird, so the extra cost would not be much. If you think you could spring for another train ticket and a few salads, it would help me avoid the marital discord that would be a sure thing if I come on your show without her. If you don't think you can pay for it, I'll scrounge up the money for somewhere; it'll be worth it in the long run.

ς

Musings on the Important Matter of Farm Gates

D ear Larry:

Now that we are sort of retired and living out on the prairie where it is real quiet, I am finding time to muse on important matters such as farm gates. We have two gates out here at the farm now, and you have to drive through both of them to get from the house out to Detour Road. It occurred to me the other day that I am doing a lot of climbing in and out of my truck . . . sorry, I mean "rig" . . . to open and close those gates as I run from here to town and back. That got me to thinking on the most efficient way to get through a gate, because over time, the time savings and wear-and-tear savings on your knees could be considerable.

As usual, Annie thinks these musing are a big waste of time and boring to everybody but me. She also thinks that being retired and having more time to contemplate life's quandaries is not necessarily improving the quality of my thinking.

Now, I am asking you to muse on this gate dilemma and let me know where you come out. I will be inter-

ested in what you have to say on this important subject. And please don't let Hotie hear what you are
musing on because I know she will not be objective
and will just side with Annie.

Anyway, I started working on two different
approaches to the gate question while our nephews,
Charlie and Mac, were visiting from back East. We got
out my old watch with the second hand on it and the
boys timed me from the back door of our house, out
to my rig, getting in, starting her up, turning her
around, driving up to the gate, getting out, opening
the gate, getting back in the rig, driving through, getting out again, closing the gate, getting back in the rig,
and driving off.

Then they timed while I tried it by walking out the
back door, walking to the gate, opening the gate,
walking back to the rig, getting in, starting her up.
(Annie, by the way, objects to my calling the rig a
"her" because she does not like the concept of a man
climbing onto a female object and turning a key to get
things going—she says a man saying something like
"starting her up" suggests general insensitivity to the
feelings of women. To that I say, "Give me a break.")
Anyway, back to the gate analysis: After I start "it"
up, I turn the rig around, drive through the gate, get
out, close the gate, get back in, and drive off.

Now, if you are following all this you will realize
that there are two important factors at work, as I said
above—time, and wear and tear on the body. The first
approach takes an average of 115 seconds to complete
while the second approach takes an average of 145
seconds to do. So there is a big difference.

But here's more to consider. In the first approach there are 31 seconds devoted to a combination of walking and climbing. While in the second approach there are 57 seconds so devoted. The second approach involved almost double the wear and tear.

There is also the matter of "gate open" time. The gate is open much longer in the second approach. The longer the gate is open, the greater the chance that an animal will escape and run off into the hinterlands where you will spend the better part of your day trying to coax it back to the farm and inside the gate so a coyote won't eat it for supper. Furthermore, the longer the gate is open, the greater the chance that the wind will blow it closed and you'll have to start all over.

So, I concluded that the first approach was clearly the better one and started doing it that way all the time. That is, until Jolie showed up for a visit last week and thought about it herself and told me that she thinks my logic is flawed. She thinks that what I call "wear and tear" the rest of the world calls "exercise" and that more exercise is better unless of course you push yourself to the point of exhaustion and start running the risk of keeling over dead from a stroke. She also does not think I am running any overexertion risk in dealing with gates.

So that has thrown a wrench into my whole way of thinking about all this and that is why I need your clear-headed analysis.

Now here is Annie looking over my shoulder again and asking why I am writing such foolishness when I could be out at the barn helping her water her animals. She says she thinks I am wasting time again and need to find something more productive to use up my meager brain capacity on—like getting a second book written and into stores so we can make some money that she can spend on getting a few more alpacas.

And by the way, she says that she is the one who gets in and out of the rig to open and close the gate when we are riding together and that if I want to analyze something, it should be on how much she does for me that I don't notice or thank her for. She thinks I should total all that up and then we'd both be shocked at all her effort and then I could pay some of it back by taking her dancing—which she says I'm good at but don't put any effort into any more.

"Oh, brother," I say.

So, anyway, where do you come out on all of this?

Best,
SAM

Behind Closed Doors

Dear Jim:

The reason I'm writing is that I was thinking about the conversation we had a few weeks ago on living in a house full of women. You were right; we are in similar boats—surrounded on all sides by wives and daughters without any other boys around to balance things out.

Last Sunday morning, Annie and I got up late and had a nice leisurely breakfast. We thought about going into town to church, but I'm afraid laziness got the better of us. Since we moved out here into the country, Annie has learned to make good coffee and often bakes chocolate almond biscotti. I have to say that I like coffee and cookies for breakfast. So we just sat at the butcher-block table in our kitchen, watched the ospreys, Olivia and Oscar, dive into the river for their breakfast, and listened to Willie Nelson on the stereo.

After breakfast, Annie pulled on her work boots and went out to the barn to feed the dogs, goats and alpacas. Shortly after she left, I retired to the bathroom with the Sunday paper and settled in.

Now I am wondering if this ever happens to you. I

couldn't have been in the bathroom more than two or three minutes before Annie comes back in from the barn. I can hear her tromping all over the house in her boots. I know she is looking for me and wondering where I've disappeared to since I am no longer at the kitchen table where she left me.

Well, some things in my life are predictable. Here it came:

"Sam, honey, where are you? I can't seem to find you," Annie yells.

I yell back, "I'm in the bathroom. I'll be out in a minute."

So, I settle back into the Sunday paper and before I get through one column, she's at the bathroom door.

"Are you okay in there?" she asks.

"Yes Annie, I'm just fine. Thank you for checking."

"I don't hear anything going on in there," she says.

"What would you like to hear?" I say.

"Well, you've been in there for a long time," she says.

"Now, why would you say that?" I reply. "You just came in from the barn two minutes ago. How could you know how long I've been in here?"

"Well, it seems like you've been in there for a long time," she says.

"Well, I have not been in here for a long time and I'll be out when I'm finished," I say with a hint of finality in my reply.

"You don't have to get snippy about it," she says. "I was just concerned about you."

"Annie, I am not trying to be snippy about it, but I am in the bathroom and would appreciate a little privacy. Unlike you, I am not inclined to conversation while sitting on the toilet. Can you just let me be for a little while? I promise I'll check in with you as soon as I'm through in here."

"Okay," she says. "I just wanted to make sure you weren't having a heart attack or something in there. You seem a little cranky. Maybe you're a little constipated."

"I'm okay," I say. "I have gone into a bathroom and closed the door every day for the last 54 years. Thus far, I have emerged unharmed every time. I know how to do this. I appreciate your concern. I am suffering from some temporary constipation because you're standing outside the bathroom door trying to start up a conversation. If you'll go about your business and let me do mine, I'm sure I'll be just fine."

It just so happens that our guest bathroom (the one I was in) is next to our laundry room. Instead of heading back out to the barn, Annie decides that this would be a good time to fold some laundry.

Hovering outside bathrooms is not an unusual occurrence in our house. Very often when I go into the bathroom and shut the door, Annie will show up just outside and do something like carry on a conversation on her cell phone. I may not normally have what you'd call magnetic qualities, but I seem to develop them whenever I go into a room and close the door.

Now, finishing your business and reading the newspaper are difficult to do with folks hovering right outside the bathroom door. So, I generally make some remark like, "Annie dear, would you mind going off somewhere else until I get out of the bathroom?" And that re-starts the conversation I just tried so hard to stop.

"I'm folding the laundry," she'll say. "I'm not trying to bother you."

Then I have to say something conciliatory like, "I know you're not trying to bother me, but I'd appreciate a little privacy."

"Well, you're in the bathroom with the door closed," she toots. "How much more privacy do you need?"

"Another room's worth," I say. "A small room is 10 feet by 12 feet. How about you move 10 to 12 feet away from the bathroom door?"

"Okay," she says. "Sorry I'm bothering you. Do you realize that you've become increasingly antisocial since we moved away from the city out to the country?"

So, here we go again. How do you end a conversation like this without going mad? I try, "You're probably right, dear. Why don't we discuss this after I get through in the bathroom?" (I'm pleading now.) "Please move away from the door and give me the privacy I so desperately crave just for a few minutes and I promise I'll talk about my shyness and general antisocial behavior as long as you'd like when I get out of here."

Now, I've noticed the same phenomenon in other situations. Shortly after we moved into our house in Seattle, I asked Annie and the girls what space in the house they considered the least habitable. They all pointed to this little room off the kitchen that nobody could figure out what to do with. So, I said, "Okay, I'll take that as my office." There were raised eyebrows all around, but, since nobody else wanted it, there wasn't any argument.

So, I set up a desk, a chair, and a file cabinet in that little room, plus a small bookcase. I loved my office. When things got a little out of hand in the house and the decibel level got too high, I could just retire to my little place. There was no room for another human being in there, so I considered it a real haven.

It got to the point where Annie and the girls could see some look pass across my face that would tip them off and they'd say something like, "We're getting ready to lose Dad; he looks like he's getting ready to go to his office for a while." And most of the time, they were right.

Well, I found out that I could go in there and be left alone as long as I didn't close the door. If I closed the door, it would only be a few minutes before one of them (let's say it was Marshall) would show up and say, through the door, "Hey Dad, are you in there?"

"Yes," I'd say.

"Are you okay in there?" Marshall would say.

"Do you hear me screaming for help?" I'd jest. "Of course I'm okay in here."

"Can I come in?" she'd say.

"Yes, you can come in," I'd reply.

The doorknob would turn and she'd stick her head in and say, "What's going on in here?"

"Not a thing," I'd say. "I'm just reading."

"Are you mad about something?" she'd say.

"No, I'm not mad about anything," I'd say.

"Are you sure?" she'd say.

"Yes, positive," I'd say.

"Well, why did you close the door then?" she'd inquire.

"Because I wanted to read in peace," I'd say.

"Are we being too loud?" she'd say.

"No, you guys are doing just fine," I'd say.

"Well, we must be doing something to irritate you or you wouldn't have the door closed," she'd say.

"No, you guys are not doing anything to irritate me. I just need a little quiet time. So, would you mind closing the door on your way out?" I'd say.

Then the door would close and I'd hear Marshall in the kitchen saying something to Annie like, "Dad's mad about something."

A few minutes would pass in relative peace before Annie would show up at the door, stick her head in, and say, "What are you mad about?"

And there we'd go again.

So what is the psychological underpinning of this behavior? I know that it's not politically correct to ask such questions, but I'm figuring you're smart enough to keep this to yourself. I'm guessing that it's the curiosity thing that gets them. If I go into a room and close the door, there must be something not quite right going on in there—emotionally or physically. I could be mad or sad or just irritated or slightly depressed. Or hiding something. Or I could be sick or having a heart attack or suffering from constipation. In any event, whatever it is, it needs clarification and must be checked up on.

So, enough on this subject. I'm interested in what

you think. Please write me back and let me have the benefit of your thinking. I promise I won't share it with anybody, including Mariette and your girls.

Best,
SAM

Where We Really Live

Dear Bob:

It was good to hear from you. Technically, you're right; we don't live in Walla Walla. Our farm is about 15 miles west of downtown Walla Walla. From here on the porch, the nearest little town is Lowden— an unincorporated village of 50 residents, if everybody's around the day you go to count. It's a sleepy little place that time has mostly passed by.

Today, Lowden is a shadow of its former self and is pretty much just a bump in the road providing a home to a couple of wineries, an irrigation supply company, a salt supply company and an in-town farm that sells pigs, chickens, cows and other assorted farm animals to whomever sees the hand-painted sign out by the highway and stops by. Just in case you're wondering, the salt company delivers field salts to farmers who want to encourage local populations of the ground-dwelling alkali bees that pollinate the alfalfa and other flowering crops here in the valley. That is a story unto itself, so I'll write you another time about bees and the important work they do out here.

As an unincorporated town, Lowden doesn't have to deal with much on its own. County officials pretty much take care of government for us. If you turned on your TV and tuned in to the local access channel, you wouldn't be likely to see anybody proposing Lowden building height limits, a leash law or road improvements.

The Lowden wineries attract tourists to town and Dunning Irrigation Supply attracts the locals. We see our neighbors and the very few Lowden townsfolk during visits to Dunning to pick up gate latches, sprinklers and seed. One of the first people we met there was Larry who was born and bred about a mile up the road. Larry is in his 70s now and is a good example of Lowden's remaining living history. I will tell you more about Larry but first I should load you up with some very interesting history on the settlement of Lowden.

As you already know, the Walla Walla Valley was home to several Indian tribes—primarily the Cayuse and Walla Walla—until the mid-1850s when the US government decided it was time to open the valley to homesteading whites and moved the Indians onto a reservation down near Pendleton in Oregon. That was a troubled time. During the Indian Wars of the 1850s, most of the whites who'd settled down in the valley after careers in the fur trade moved to avoid losing their hair to the local Indians who were (not surprisingly) a little upset about being relocated from the place they called home onto a reservation they didn't.

So, it wasn't until the late 1850s and early 1860s that white folks moved back in and started farming around here. That's when Larry's great grandfather—a fellow named Francis Lowden, Sr.—arrived.

Apparently, Francis had a tough time living with his older brother after helping him establish a ranch in northern California, so Francis started a mule-based pack train business to take advantage of the California gold rush. As that gold rush started to fall off, the Northwest gold rush started up, and Francis moved his mule business to the Walla Walla Valley.

From here he packed mining and other supplies into Idaho, Montana and Oregon mining camps. At one point, he was running 125 mules from Columbia River ports into those mining camps.

In 1869, Francis gave up the pack train business and bought 160 acres (for $10 per acre) at the intersection of the Walla Walla River and Dry Creek (which is not always dry). Having helped his brother set up a ranch in California, Francis was familiar with the importance of water to the success of any agricultural endeavor in dry, sunny places.

Beyond water, the big issue for anybody farming or ranching in these parts was transportation—a reliable means of moving produce and livestock to markets out on the western coast where there were enough hungry people to buy the fruits of their labor. Fortunately, good karma suffused the valley and provided the gold rush to save the day for local farmers.

A gold rush was an interesting phenomenon. You know the story: Gold-hungry panners would get wind of opportunity and stampede toward any area of the west promising pay dirt. And that's what happened around here. Now, before you run out to buy a pie tin and get on a bus to Walla Walla to seek your fortune, you should know that there wasn't any gold around here. (At least we haven't found any yet.)

No, Walla Walla didn't promise gold, but it offered mild winters and mining supplies to mountain claim diggers who found the winter snows and cold winds in Idaho and Montana a little outside their comfort zone. As the gold rush developed, Walla Walla became home to those who sold picks, shovels and food to over-wintering miners. The merchants needed a way to get their picks and shovels delivered from the coast to Walla Walla, so other enterprising folks, like Francis Lowden, started running supplies up the Columbia River to Wallula (the former site of the Hudson Bay trading post on the bank of the mighty Columbia) and from there overland up the Walla Walla Valley into town. On their way out, they hauled produce and live-stock to those west coast markets I mentioned.

Local farmers and ranchers who had access to water and a way to get their products to market could now make a go of it and the best of them did pretty well. That meant that Larry's great grandfather Lowden had found himself a good spot. He raised cattle, ran a dairy, and made butter and cheese. He and his wife, Mary, also raised three kids.

In the 1870s a church was established on the Walla Walla River about five miles east of present day Lowden. It became the center of life for the area dubbed "Frenchtown" because of all the French Cana-dian families that had congregated in the valley between Wallula and Walla Walla. Sometime in the 1880s, after a railroad had been built through the val-ley to move goods the roughly thirty miles from the Columbia River to Walla Walla more quickly, a rail siding was put in several miles to the west of that church and called "Raymo" in honor of Narcisse Ray-mond, a former employee of the Hudson Bay Com-pany, who owned land near the site. Some years later, around 1900, that siding was moved west onto Lowden ranch property and was renamed Lowden to mark its location.

As the story goes, the railroad got the name wrong when it put up the first siding marker saying "Louden." That's when Larry's great grandmother, Mary Lowden, got ahold of local rail officials and threatened to take the land back if they didn't fix it. She said they couldn't use the name if they couldn't spell it. The next day a new sign announcing "Lowden" replaced the old one. So, the seeds of a small rural community were sown.

During the early 1900s, Lowden grew from a railroad siding into a real town. There were a one-room schoolhouse, a confectionary, a country store with a dance hall upstairs, a butcher shop, a small hotel, a post office, a hardware store, a blacksmith shop and, of course, grain elevators next to the railroad tracks. By 1915, things were going so well that the townsfolk had to build a bigger schoolhouse—one with two classrooms. That schoolhouse still stands today, converted into one of the town's two resident wineries.

According to Larry, Saturday night dances in the dance hall above the country store often went well into the wee hours of Sunday morning because local folks who rode dirt roads on horseback to get into town from area farms—many of them fording the Walla Walla River along the way—were intent on getting their money's worth for all that effort.

So, let me go back to Lowden family history for a minute. Mary and Francis Lowden's kids grew up, married, and had children. One of these children was a girl named Mary Irene who later married a boy named Paul whose family (including nine children) had moved to the valley to escape a Kansas drought that turned their farm there into a dustbowl. Mary Irene and Paul had one son, Lawrence Lowden Dodd, who was born in 1935. Larry grew up on the Lowden family ranch.

Larry went to the local school until ninth grade when he had to leave Lowden and go into Walla Walla to attend high school, a place where all the boys were involved in one of two extracurricular activities—the school band or the school ROTC program. Larry is not musically inclined, apparently flunked Introduction to the Plastic Flute, and therefore ended up in ROTC.

He went on to Washington State College (before it became a university) in Pullman, Washington, graduated in 1957 and enlisted in the Air Force where he became an aircraft mechanic and spent a year in Korea.

While he was stationed in Korea, he and several friends started visiting an orphanage near the base and spending time with the kids. It was a rewarding time for Larry. As his tour of duty in Korea ended and Larry boarded the plane to leave, he looked down the runway and saw well over a hundred kids from the orphanage there waving to him—bidding him farewell. It still brings tears to his eyes when he tells the story.

Before Larry could complete his military commitment, the Cuban Missile Crisis intervened and extended his military stay for a few extra months. But soon the crisis subsided; Larry was discharged; and he drove straight home to his beloved Lowden. Shortly after he arrived back home, his father died.

Thereafter, Larry did whatever he had to do to stay in Lowden and on the family ranch. He didn't want to be a farmer, so he and his mother leased the farm to another local farming family while Larry pursued other employment. He monitored wheat and barley planting for the government, managed parks for the Corps of Engineers and, after a Corps personnel cutback, found a half-time job working at the Whitman Mission museum—site of the famous mission where missionaries Marcus and Narcissa Whitman set up shop back in 1836. There he found that he loved learning about local history.

In the non-working half of his life, he started collecting information on his own family history. For the next five years, he taught local history to Whitman Mission visitors and dove into the archives at the Penrose Memorial Library at Whitman College where townsfolk have always been welcome. Hour after hour he read through old papers, microfiche and books on the history of the Northwest, searching for ever more information to put into his personal history scrapbooks. And that's when the door opened for Larry.

I'm not trying to get gummy on you here, but I guess you never know when you'll be given an opportunity to discover the work that gives a person's life on this earth meaning. You never know when circumstances will conspire to change the path of a life. But the door did open for Larry and he walked right through it.

After five years of studying archived material at the Whitman College library, getting to know the staff, and becoming a fixture around the place, Larry was tapped to run the library's first floor which included the library's local, regional and Pacific Northwest archives. They not only handed Larry the cookie jar, they put him in it. It was 1969; the Vietnam War was in full swing; college campuses were getting restless; and Sam McLeod was just graduating from high school.

For the next 35 years, Larry whittled down his job description and focused on his life's love—building a world class history archives for students and towns-folk alike.

In June of 2003, Larry retired as Archivist Emeritus of Whitman College and handed over the archive keys to the new full-time archivist. He's only been back twice—finding it too hard to be there and have to walk away again.

He tells a good story about being at the library one day years ago and getting a phone call from the Walla Walla City Manager who explained to Larry that the old firehouse was going to be torn down. The city fathers had apparently discovered a small storage room sitting out on the second floor roof of the firehouse full of "old papers." The City Manager wanted to know if Larry wanted them before they threw them out.

So, Larry hotfooted it down to the old firehouse with two Whitman students in tow, loaded up his truck and saved a bunch of boxes full of papers from the trash heap. Well, it took a while to look through them back at the library, but he soon discovered that the boxes were full of public records containing, among other things, minutes of the first meeting of the Walla Walla City Council, hundreds of original deeds, and several volumes of birth and death records.

He was holding what were clearly public records and wanted to know what to do with them. So he called the public records archivist for the State of Washington. Well, the archivist was out of town for a few days, so he talked to the archivist's assistant who listened patiently to Larry's story and then lit into him, telling him that he'd absconded with public records in violation of the law and that the state was going to sue Larry and Whitman College for the theft.

Larry passed a very uncomfortable few days waiting for a call back from the state archivist who did in fact call and apologize for the behavior of his assistant whose zeal had outstripped his common sense. In the end, the documents were returned to the city for safekeeping and Larry did not spend the rest of his life in jail.

Larry still lives on the family place—the one his great grandfather Lowden settled—in a town carrying his family name. He keeps up the house and barn where generations of the Lowden clan have lived, and tinkers with the farm equipment—once a mechanic, always a mechanic. He's a man who never married and never had any children of his own, but now helps raise his neighbors' ten-year-old son four days a week while his parents bring home the bacon. The boy calls him "Grandpa."

Larry spent thirty-five years at Whitman College pursuing the work that consumed and satisfied him. And he still works occasionally on his own Lowden history volumes—several hundreds, maybe now thousands, of pages that, he says, require a little more research and writing. My guess is that Larry will never consider that work finished.

So, I hope I haven't bored you to death with the history lesson but that is what I know about Lowden—the place where we really live. Getting to know those who've lived here all their lives has been one of the real pleasures of moving to the country. The history is interesting, particularly when it's your neighbors who made it.

Best,
SAM

Chicago . . . Here Comes Walla Walla . . . Sorry About That . . .

Dear Oprah:

I don't know whether you got my last letter yet, but I need to get your guidance on how you want to handle your show featuring my book called *Welcome to Walla Walla*. A couple of days ago, I told Floyd that Annie was saying that she is going to make the trip to Chicago with us, come hell or high water. So, now Floyd is saying that his wife Mary is making noises about coming along and that his daughter, Mary (I call her Mary Jr.), and her husband, Jon, may want to come since they were characters in the book, too.

If that was all there was to it, I wouldn't feel so bad, but apparently they have mentioned it to a few folks in town and I'm now getting calls from Bob and Kelly and Cowboy Bob and the other Bob and Jeffrey and, well, several of the Larrys and a few other folks (about 34 the last time I looked at the list) who are all saying that they think your show will not be complete without them.

Before I forget, Kelly also wanted me to ask you if regular people have ever been on your show and then gone on to be big movie stars.

Anyway, yesterday there was a letter to the editor in the *Walla Walla Union-Bulletin* saying that the writer ("Larry from Walla Walla") had gotten wind of our Chicago trip to be on "Oprah." He thinks that an author who is a positive influence in the community would not exclude other folks in town from going to Chicago for free to be on your show. I think he was saying that if Floyd and Annie and I go to Chicago without the other folks in town who want to be there too, he and other Walla Wallans will not think kindly of me and might not be inclined to buy my books in the future—but maybe I'm just being a little paranoid.

It occurred to me that this could be a bad thing and that if this Chicago trip gets me off on the wrong foot with long-time Walla Wallans, it could make my career as an up-and-coming author more of a get-out-of-town kind of experience.

Anyway, I have been thinking that there's a better way to handle this. After you've thought about it, why don't you decide who (in addition to Floyd and Annie and me, of course) you want to invite and then I can tell other folks that I tried to get them an invitation but that you didn't want them to come. If you don't mind taking the heat, it'd be a big help to me.

Alternatively, you could bring your whole film crew and make-up people and all out here to Walla Walla to do the show and we could let the whole town know the date and folks could come or not as they see fit.

That way we could both be good guys and keep our popularity up.

Okay then, please think on that and let me know your druthers. Annie says to say "hi," and Floyd is poking me in the ribs to ask you if he'll have to wear make-up, which he is willing to do if that's the only way you'll let him on the show, but he'd rather not have to, just so you know.

Best,
SAM

Neighbors

D ear Bahlman:

I have just figured out the problem I've been dealing with most every morning out here on the farm: Modern store-bought bread just doesn't fit in toasters circa 1975. Every morning, Annie and I get up at the crack of dawn and do our chores for an hour or so before we get our breakfast. Somehow I've managed to take on all the cooking duties around here. Annie says I'm a better cook than she is and that she likes having somebody waiting on her, three meals a day. She says it's one of the many ways I demonstrate my affection and undying love for her, which, she says, is only appropriate given that I won't go dancing with her. I'm not sure I'm following that train of thinking, but however you want to think about it, I do the cooking.

Anyway, I've noticed this toast thing and have been wondering about it. I'm thinking that the toast people and the toaster people have gotten together and decided that folks with aging toasters need to get new ones. Thus far, I'm not bending to the pressure even though Annie is starting to side with them.

Our toaster is the one we got as a wedding present now thirty years ago. It works just fine except that modern sliced bread doesn't fit in it. I shove the new, wider-than-square pieces of bread into our old, square-holed toaster knowing that there's no way the toast will pop up on its own when it's done. After the toaster tries, but fails, to eject our toast, I have to unplug the toaster and fish around in the guts of the thing with a knife until the toast comes loose. The toast emerges a little beat up and there are crumbs all over the counter top where I've been fighting with the machine, but all in all it's fine. To my way of thinking, toast is toast.

Now Annie says we're starting to have folks come and stay in the cottage and they'll be coming over to the house for coffee and toast in the morning. She thinks it'd be nice if we served better looking toast; she says our bent toast distracts folks from enjoying the good coffee and jams she makes. Well, that might be right but I still think that our toast is good enough and that we shouldn't be letting the toast and toaster crowd bully us into buying a new toaster that we don't really need.

I remind Annie that we're now committed to frugality and conservation and that we shouldn't be running out to buy a new toaster when ours works fine. We can save the earth and money at the same time and feel good about it. She says that my way of thinking works just fine for most things but not for things she wants, particularly when the comfort of our guests is at stake.

If this little battle gets resolved the way most of our marital disagreements do, I'm guessing that there'll be a new toaster under the Christmas tree for me this year. So the best I can hope for is to avoid paying for a new toaster until December.

Anyway, that's not what I started to write you about. I was going to tell you about our neighbors. Now, I know you're thinking that I'm getting ready to bore you with a few superficial facts about our human neighbors down along Detour Road. Well, I'm not. There are interesting folks down the way, but they're so far away that you can't really call them neighbors—at least not in the city sense. No, I'm going to tell you about our close-in feathered neighbors—the ones we see most every day.

Olivia and Oscar

About two weeks ago, new neighbors moved in on the riverfront—a nesting pair of ospreys. According to Annie, their names are Olivia and Oscar. (I know what you are thinking; and I'm telling you that there's no point in asking. Those are their names and that's just the way it is.)

They arrived sometime late on a Wednesday, so we first saw them the following Thursday morning. Oscar is an early bird and starts fishing when the first rays of sunlight pass over the Blue Mountains and land in the river bottom. Olivia is a bit of a homebody and tends to sit on a dead branch above the water near their huge nest while she squawks at Oscar to hurry up and get breakfast. She seems a little cranky, which Annie attributes to her upcoming egg laying duties.

I guess they were here last year, but we wouldn't know because we weren't. I can only imagine that they arrived back at their Walla Walla summer home on that Wednesday night and found that we were squatting on their property in what looked to be a very permanent sort of way.

I don't think Olivia was very happy about our moving in and seemed to be on Oscar to say something to us about moving on. So Oscar spent his first few days back in Walla Walla flying over the house and our little menagerie of dogs, alpacas and goats squawking his head off and making it very clear with his body language (mostly pooping on everything he could target) that we were unwelcome. "Kill 'em with kindness," Annie said. So, we'd all just wave to Oscar as he dive-bombed us and act like we appreciated his attention.

Now, I'm beginning to think that our "pleasant neighbor" policy is working. Yesterday, while I was sitting on the front porch pretending to read the newspaper, Oscar flew up and perched on the fence post next to the woodpile with a small fish in his claws. At first I thought it was a house-warming gift, but found out pretty quickly that he was just sneaking a little snack for himself out of Olivia's sight. I drank my coffee while he ate his sashimi and we had a right nice time looking at each other. Once you get to know Oscar, you find out that he's sort of the strong silent type—not a lot to say but a nice enough guy to have around.

Annie's pretty sure that Olivia will calm down after the babies are born and her hormones return to normal. Annie loves babies and thinks that Olivia will not be able to resist the urge to bring them over and show them off. Meanwhile, we get great pleasure out of watching their antics around the nest and still haven't gotten over their fishing prowess. They are regularly catching fish in stretches of the river where Annie and I regularly catch nothing.

Henrietta

Henrietta, the great blue heron, is still hanging out in the field just outside the fence near the big pile of rocks and dirt that represent the beginnings of our new root cellar. (Adam calls us every few weeks to explain the latest delay in the project. He knows we're in no hurry. I guess that makes us even—a true Walla Walla meeting of the minds.)

Anyway, Henrietta is there in the field most days from late morning until early afternoon. I'm guessing that the fishing slows down under the mid-day sun and that there are better opportunities in mouse hunting out in the field. According to Mike, our Forest Service friend, we have an impressive number of voles in that field.

With some regularity we see Henrietta standing heron-still, eyeing movement in the grass at her feet. She looks like she is frozen in mid-stride until she makes her move with lightening speed and nails one of

those little microtines (the fancy name for voles). Between meals, Henrietta takes short catnaps—asleep on her feet.

I asked Mike why Henrietta seemed to be so comfortable in the middle of the field with coyotes nosing around in her mousing territory from time to time. Apparently, heron are very smart creatures and have learned that coyotes value their eyesight—in fact coyotes have a very tough time making it in the wild without their eyesight. Heron have learned that pecking out the occasional coyote eye is a good deterrent to intrusion. Coyotes are quick studies, so they just leave the heron alone.

We are pretty sure Henrietta has no mate in her life. If she does, she's hiding him. I say it is no surprise to me because Henrietta is sort of a stern figure and spends most of her non-working hours sleeping or looking down her long beak at the rest of the world. I think she's a little stuck on herself, lacking in social skills, and therefore probably hard to live with. I should also tell you that, when she flies, she makes a noise much like the worst kind of nose blowing you've ever heard. I'm guessing potential suitors find this a somewhat unattractive habit. Annie is a much kinder soul and says maybe Henrietta is just shy and has learned to hide her discomfort in social settings by playing the wallflower.

Sam 3

Our nearest neighbor to the south is Sam 3, the

Northern Harrier—a kind of hawk. Everybody asks us why we call him Sam 3. It's a too-long story and not worth going into unless you have absolutely nothing left to do in your life.

Sam 3 was here all last summer and spent a good bit of his time watching our new house being built. He'd grab a field mouse and savor his meal while sitting on a corner of our new roof, watching the carpenters frame up the walls. He took off early in the fall headed for South America and we figured that would be the last time we'd see him. But, here he is again this summer, staking out his fence post perches and occasionally calling out to us as we walk by with what sounds more like a scream than a greeting. His female friend is new to us; we just figured out a week or so ago that they were a couple. We learned from our bird book that these hawks nest on the ground. Given that we consistently see them in the same spot every day, we're guessing that there's a nest in the fence line hidden in the brush somewhere.

Phinney

Last but not least there is philandering Phinney, the ring-necked pheasant, who has taken up a "crowing territory" just outside the fence east of the house. In the last few days, he has collected quite a bevy of female friends. Phinney has staked out roughly an acre, and can be down right rude to anybody (including us) intruding upon his space. We regularly watch Phinney, and the five other males in their territories

surrounding Phinney, strutting around in self-impor-
tance and beating their wings in such a way as to
sound much like playing cards clothes-pinned to the
spokes of a fast-turning bicycle wheel.

Now, we can't figure out exactly why, but Phinney has
attracted five female pheasants to his little corner of the
world right in front of our house while the other males
have one or two mates at most. Annie thinks Phinney's
been lying to his ladies—telling them that those other
guys are full of hot air and lacking in substance while he
has a nice new house (our house) and a big rig (mine)
parked in the driveway. I don't know what he's offered
them but, whatever his story, he does have quite the nice
little harem. Or, at least he used to . . .

This morning I woke up with the sun. I could see
Phinney from the comfort of our bed—strutting
around, crowing at everything that moved, and beating his wings while his harem pecked at our grass seed
in the dirt at their feet and largely ignored him. All the
sudden, he took off and raided the territory of another
male nearby. Feathers flew and, after awhile, Phinney
returned with a new female to add to his stable.

It took him a few minutes, but he finally figured out
that, during his absence, two of his harem had wandered off to the territory of another male just over the
small ridge. He'd started out with five females and all
his effort had netted him four. This made Phinney
mad.

So, what did he do? He took off after another male
and grabbed his only female. When he returned with
her, he discovered that all four of his former harem

had moved in with the guy just below the alpaca pasture. He'd started that raid with four females and all his effort had netted him one. This really made Phinney mad.

So, what did he do? He took off after the guy who was shacked up with his four former lovers, lost the battle, and returned to find that his one remaining female had disappeared into the willows down by the river. Phinney was suddenly harem-less. Greedy, greedy, greedy . . .

I don't know what happened after that. I got up to take a shower, but before I left our bedroom I had to tell this story to Annie who was still half asleep. She said Phinney reminded her of a guy she knew in high school—one of those guys who could have had any girl in town, wanted them all, and ended up with none. As far as she knows, this guy never married and has therefore led a predictably miserable life. She thinks Phinney and this guy have a lot in common and that Phinney should take a lesson from this story but probably won't.

So, basically Annie thinks Phinney needs to settle down with one very nice young pheasantess who will devote her life to straightening him out.

Anyway, enough about the neighbors. As you can tell, they're a lot like human neighbors with their human-like little dramas . . . Better go. Annie is out in the car beeping the horn; I think she wants to go buy a new toaster.

Best,
SAM

Drinking Wine

Dear Reader: This letter is addressed to some more Larrys . . . I know a lot of Larrys . . . and other folks who are always pestering me to write letters to them so they can stay in my books and ensure their continuing fame. I am killing a lot of birds with this one stone—so to speak.

Dear Brad, Bob, Horst, Cliff, Dave, Tony, Chad, Larry, Larry, Buck, Tom, Frank, Gary and Randy:

I am sitting out on the porch right now writing to you guys. As you can see, I am counting on this letter to catch me up on a lot of correspondence.

It is one of those cool, overcast days around here. All last night and early this morning, it rained to beat the band, so the big meadow out in front of the house is wet and full of life. It rains so little out here on the prairie that a little moisture is cause for celebration among the farmers, feathered creatures, and bugs who live out this way. Crickets are chirping down by the river, the frogs are croaking and the swallows are out in full force gobbling up any poor little gnat that leaves the protection of the tall grasses that have grown up around us.

Phinney, the pheasant, is standing on the pile of dirt

by the big hole in the ground where our root cellar is patiently waiting on Adam to show up and build it. Phinney is still crowing his head off and beating his wings hoping to get a girl pheasant to come into his territory for a little afternoon delight, but as far as I can tell the lady pheasants have had enough of Phinney and are setting on their nests waiting for the little ones to hatch.

Annie is off to Idaho to talk to a lady who wants to make blankets out of Annie's alpaca fleece. A shearer is coming out to the farm next Sunday to shear her alpacas. Once Annie has cleaned the fleeces and bagged them up, she'll send them off to be spun into yarn. She'll take some of the yarn to a lady here in Walla Walla and send the rest off to the lady in Idaho. They'll make some sample blankets, which should be back here at the farm for us to see by late summer. If all goes according to plan (which it never does around here), she will then gear up to make more alpaca blankets next year to sell in shops here in Walla Walla.

I figure the worst that happens is we get new blankets for our beds. Maybe your better halves are in the market for a new, very soft, very pretty blanket? I'm sure Annie would be glad to take early orders.

Several of you asked about Spring Release weekend when all the wineries around here show off their new wines. Here's a report:

Last Thursday night, Annie and I sat out here on the porch with a big fire blazing away in the fireplace while we watched the setting sun color the pastures and trees along the river emerald green and then a deep purple.

As it gets dark out here, you begin to see the lights on the windmills to the south and houses off on the mountaintops in the Blue Mountains to the east. Most nights, the only airplane you see is the commuter plane from Seattle that gets in about 9:00pm. You can pretty much set your watch by it. But last Thursday night the Walla Walla sky was full up with small jets and single engine airplanes ferrying folks in for the big weekend. The word on the street was that there were no rooms to be had within an hour's drive of here.

By Friday afternoon, downtown Walla Walla was buzzing with tourists hanging out at all the local watering holes and coffee shops. The town was all dressed up—American flags lining the streets and Spring Release banners flying from all the street lamps.

The downtown wine tasting rooms were open and filled to overflowing with wine samplers. I overheard one of the visitors say that the wineries out near the airport were swamped with folks who'd flown into town and gone straight to Tamarack, Buty, and all the other wineries located just off the runway.

We went out to dinner at Creek Town Café late Friday night with friends in from Seattle. Tom, the head greeter, sat down and had a bite of dessert with us as things slowed down around 10pm. He said they'd been booked through the weekend for months.

On Saturday, I did novice author book signings at Reininger Winery in the morning and at Isenhower Cellars in the afternoon.

Chuck and the rest of the Reininger clan were at their brand new winery facility just a couple of miles down the road from our place, greeting visitors arriving on foot, by car and even helicopter—an unusual way to tour wine country offering lots of noise, blowing dust and dismounts that scream "notice me, notice me." Chuck had set up two well-stocked tables for wine tasters and several other tables overflowing with cheeses, fruit, cakes and fresh-brewed coffees. Artwork was hung from wine barrels stacked high in the barrel room and artists strolled among the gathered to talk about their work. I sat perched on a stool by the coffee table, signed a few books and talked with folks from as far away as my hometown, Nashville.

Chuck and his family put on quite a show. When you get here for one of these big wine weekends, we'll definitely go by. The wines are fabulous and the people are welcoming.

About mid-afternoon I scooted over to Isenhower Cellars, a small winery where Brett and Denise make some of our favorite syrahs. It's interesting to see how these events reflect the personalities of their hosts and hostesses. Brett and Denise are very casual and friendly. Their three dogs roam free around the winery greeting newcomers but mostly looking for handouts from guests gathered around tables piled high with food. I don't know how much wine they sold that day but the crowds were impressive.

The late-afternoon crowd was predictably bleary-eyed after a full day's tasting, but still enjoying the party. It was nice for me that, by late in the day, many of the ladies in the crowd had had enough of wine and were looking for something else to do while their husbands and boyfriends continued their swilling. You won't believe me, but those poor ladies were so tired of wine that talking to me was more inviting than another glass of spirits. If they'd really had any choice, I'm guessing that a nap would have been first on their list.

Given that I was busy most of the day peddling my book, Annie spent the day with Greg and Linda touring wineries; we had dinner at their house Saturday night. We cooked some chicken on the grill, sat out on their patio, and drank a bottle of Ash Hollow Somanna—a breezy warm evening made for picnic dinners.

On Sunday morning, Annie and I hopped in the rig and drove into town to meet Jolie at Coffee Connection for breakfast. Thank goodness we went a little early because by 9:00am there was a line out the door of folks drinking black coffee and pining away for a big breakfast to calm their acid-etched stomachs. The combination of Mother's Day and a town full of wine buyers was creating some real people jams everywhere you looked.

After breakfast, Jolie and Annie went off to look at some of Jolie's new artwork. I headed out toward the airport to Tamarack Cellars where Ron was doing his best to keep up with an overflow crowd. After I dropped off a few books and waved goodbye over the heads of folks lined up five and six deep around the wine pourers, I drove on out Mill Creek Road past the Inn at Abeja where uniformed patrolmen were directing traffic in and out of the winery. While we've always got a cottage room for you guys, you might want to think about staying at the Inn for a night or two. It is a beautiful place—a completely restored farmhouse and outbuildings all converted into some of the nicest bedroom suites you've ever seen. They serve a great breakfast and their first-class winery is just steps from your bedroom door.

Anyway, I kept trucking out to Walla Walla Vintners. Gordy and Myles are the winemakers. Gordy tells me that they started out life as the seventh or eighth winery in the Walla Walla Valley. The winery is in a renovated barn out at the foot of the Blue Mountains on top of a hill where the views are unbelievable. Gordy's office upstairs looks out over the entire Walla Walla Valley.

Gordy and Myles have been around so long that the crowd—mostly of old friends—was there that morning as much to see them and their families as to drink wine. I met lots of folks who bought their first bottle of Walla Walla Vintners wine back in the early days and have been back every year since.

By mid-afternoon Sunday, the crowd dwindled down to a handful and I was ready to call it a day. Drinking coffee, signing some books and gabbing with the guests can really wear a guy down.

As I started to say my goodbyes, here came the locals. I hadn't really noticed it until then, but I hadn't seen many familiar faces during the weekend. Turns out local Walla Wallans are very smart folks; they know the visitors are going to get in their cars, planes and helicopters, and head back to where they came from by early Sunday afternoon. So, they just hunker down at home most of the weekend and wait their turn. Late Sunday afternoon the wineries fill up with folks again—mostly folks you know. And that's when the real party begins . . . .

Well, I'm sure I've now told you way more than you bargained for, but maybe this'll help get you all over here the first weekend in May next year. Tell your better halves that we say "hi."

Best,
ŞAM

Buns of Steel

Dear Char:

I know you haven't read *Welcome to Walla Walla* yet and I'm sure you're keeping up a good stream of excuses to feed me as I pester you about it, but you, more than most, will appreciate this. One of the stories in the book is about an impromptu contest that happened in The Oasis Restaurant and Bar one morning several months ago where, long story short, my butt was judged second best in the bar. Now, there's a lot more to this story, but that's all I'm telling you until you read the book. I just thought you'd appreciate hearing what that little story has done for me in helping me to meet new folks over here in Walla Walla; and I know how you are always on Ed to exercise more so he can get a nice looking rear end like mine.

Anyway, I went into the bookstore here the other day to check on book sales. Janice saw me and said I should maybe bring them a few more books—that in spite of my poor marketing skills the occasional person was wandering in to ask about "that new book."

Folks don't seem to know who wrote it—mostly because I used the pen name "Sam" and have managed to confuse everybody. Janice tells me that if you use a pen name, you're not supposed to tell everybody that's what you're doing because the reason for using a pen name is to hide your identity. She says using the pen name and then telling folks you did it just because you like the name is confusing to folks who read books and who would be happier if they were just dealing with one person.

So, I guess learning how to be a famous author has its ups and downs.

Anyway, she goes on to tell me that she has not read the book either but has heard about the "Best Butt Contest" story in the book from bookstore customers and that I now have the most prominent posterior in Walla Walla County. Well, I thought, if you can't be a best selling author at least you can be famous for something and I guess having a famous backside is not all bad. I found myself growing a little bit proud of my behind, until . . .

The next day I was walking down Main Street when a nice lady of a certain age stops me and says, "Hey, are you the guy that wrote that Walla Walla book?"

So, I say, "Yes, I wrote it. Have you read it?"

And she says, "No, gracious, honey; I don't have time to read the newspaper; what makes you think I'd have time to read your book?"

She goes on to say, "Hazel told me that story about the Butt Contest in your book and I'm wondering if I can check out your butt to see what all the fuss is about."

Well, I was a little surprised, but any attention is better than none I figured, so I said "sure," and turned around so she could get a look. Then she says, "Okay, honey, I've seen it. That's enough for me. I still don't know what all the chatter is about." And she just strolled on by saying, "I sure hope your book is better than your tush. If you have a day job, maybe you should hang on to it."

So, on Saturday I walked into Merchants to get a cup of coffee and do some writing when another lady of advanced years stopped me and said, "Bob tells me you're they guy who wrote that book. Is he just playing with me or is that right?"

"Yep, that's right" I say. "Did you like it?"

"It was pretty good," she says. "You don't look like what I thought you'd look like. Can I check out your backside?"

"Sure you can," I say, and turned so she could get a look.

Now, I've never had any attention like this before and I found myself thinking that when you are showing somebody your butt, you should strike some kind of model-like pose. Then I realized that I haven't the faintest idea what kind of pose that is, and that learning about posing your popo would require some further study. I mean, you can't be walking around showing your butt to folks without doing it gracefully. If I can't be a famous author, and only have my buttocks to work with, I need to learn how to show them the right way.

Anyway, the lady goes on to say she thinks Annie was right in that story and that a score of 3.4 out of a possible 10 points is about right for my butt—maybe a little generous. It is taking a little while to sink in but I'm beginning to think that she's not necessarily paying me a compliment.

So, I told Annie about her comments and what the other lady had said. After she quit laughing out loud, she told me she thinks those ladies are just shining me on and having a little fun at my expense.

"But," Annie says, "if you want to get serious about this steel buns stuff, you need to be taking long walks with me; and if all this silliness about your butt will make you get serious about exercise, I'm okay with it."

So, there it is. If I want to be sure that I can proudly display my rear end, I have to learn the right poses and take up butt firming exercises, which Annie is always on me to do anyway—not to improve my physique, mind you, but to keep me from falling over from a heart attack before my time. Who would haul the alpacas' hay around if I keeled over?

Now, since that second lady stopped me, three more women have asked to see my rear. That has got Annie thinking that, in addition to the long walks, I should take her dancing because dancing is extra good for firming up butt cheeks. I am not buying into that one; she is forever trying to get me to go dancing and has never mentioned before that it would be good for my derrière.

So far, Annie and other folks have recommended

walking, yoga, dancing, abdominal crunches, butt tucks, vitamins and a strict diet of vegetables, fish and something called essential oils. This is all starting to sound like a lot of work.

I am thinking that I'll just have a salad for lunch today and hope that that'll take care of it.

Anyway, I will keep you posted on my progress. Even if I never become a famous author, maybe I can parlay this butt attention into a spot in the next "calendar men" calendar they do for charity down in Milton-Freewater. I'm always saying that a man should try to keep his options open.

Best,
SAM

More Morels, Please

Dear Debbie:

I just opened your email and looked through the pictures you sent of your trip to New Zealand. All I can say is, "Wow." I don't know whether it was New Zealand or your camera, but those are some of the most stunningly beautiful pictures I've ever seen. I only have one suggestion. If you can do it without hurting his feelings, I'd cut back on the number of photographs featuring Scott. Until I looked through your pictures, I'd never really noticed how much he detracts from the scenery.

Summer has been here for the last week visiting until she heads off to be a summer camp counselor in New Hampshire. Annie was busy keeping one-year-old Evi for Sarah on Friday, so Sarah could get her gardening caught up. Annie seems to be enjoying her grandma training.

That left Summer and me free to plan a dad/daughter day. Summer is big on the outdoors and said she wanted to go fishing. So we gathered up our gear and headed down to Weston where we stopped at the

Long Branch Café & Saloon for breakfast before heading on over to the Wallowa River for the day. Our waitress' name was Bonnie and she had no trouble identifying us as non-Westoners. After she took our orders, she asked where we were headed and Summer proceeded to tell her about our dad/daughter fishing day.

That's when Bonnie admitted that she'd figured us for morel hunters—that folks were driving in from all over to hunt the mushrooms. Now, I've eaten morels and I love 'em but I've never hunted them. Neither Summer nor I had any idea how to hunt them, or when, or where.

As Bonnie walked back to the kitchen, Summer piped up and said she'd always wanted to hunt mushrooms and had known a couple in Charlottesville that trekked cross country hunting edible fungi and writing articles for magazines and newspapers to fund their travels. "Maybe we should ask Bonnie about hunting them so we can look for them on our hike into the river," she said.

When Bonnie came back to our table, I up and asked her, "If a couple of neophytes wanted to go morel hunting, how would we learn about it? Who would we talk to?"

"I'd be a good start," she says. "Been doing it all my life."

And the elderly couple at the next table—who couldn't help but overhear or so they said—started scooting their chairs over to our table claiming that they'd hunted morels all their lives too. They introduced themselves as Pat and Bob. Pat moved their breakfast plates and silverware over to our table while Bob went out to their truck to get his map saying that there was no way to talk intelligently about morel hunting without his map. Bonnie asked Rachel, who was helping out in the kitchen, to cover for her while she helped us get our mushroom hunting lesson. When Miss Mae and her friend Rose, who were sitting at the counter, heard that, they got up and came over saying that there was a really good place their husbands had gone a week ago and had come back with a potato sack full.

It was about then that Rachel delivered our breakfast and poured coffee all around for the assembling crowd. While Rose quizzed Summer about where we were from and what had possessed us to move out to Walla Walla when our families were "back East," and where her boyfriend was, and where his family was from, and how they'd met, and what were their plans, and Miss Mae kept trying to get Rose to give it a rest and let Summer alone, Bob got the map spread out on the table with help from Pat and Bonnie who managed to move my breakfast out of reach so I could get the map in front of me which they claimed was hard to read unless you had bifocals. Whew!

With apparent expertise based on years of experience, Rose managed to maneuver Summer closer to her where she could continue her assault on McLeod family history with help from Miss Mae who was finding our history more interesting than she'd expected and was no longer trying to shield Summer from Rose's probing. As those three moved to the fringes, Bonnie got up and came around to sit next to me while Bob and Pat stood behind us peering at the map that none of us could read very well. I'd just gotten some of those new trifocals that look like regular glasses and spent several seconds squinting at the fine print before I realized that I could see better if I just took them off.

When Pat saw my new glasses lying on the table she concluded that the problem was dust and took them off with her to find her purse because she had just gone to the new eye doctor down in Pendleton and he'd given her this magic cloth that'd clean up my glasses in a jiffy.

So now Summer was eating breakfast with her new friends Rose and Miss Mae, while I was sitting with Bob and Bonnie, but without my breakfast or my daughter or my glasses, looking at a map I couldn't read with or without glasses, guided by two folks who couldn't see the map any better than I could.

Bonnie and Bob were running their fingers all over the map trying to find the turn off to Jubilee Lake up above Tollgate, which they said was just 30 minutes up the road. Pat showed up with my newly cleaned glasses and said, "Okay there, honey; see how they do now," and promptly dropped them in my coffee. Whereupon she struck off again—this time to the bathroom—to wash my glasses before she used her magic cloth on them again.

Bonnie finally found the turnoff to Jubilee Lake and she and Bob debated the merits of going all the

way up to the lake or just going to up to the meadows below Bald Mountain. It seems that morel growth is a function of temperature, moisture and soil conditions. According to Bob, our mild and very dry winter has really thrown the morels for a loop; so this year folks are chucking the old rules about where and when to hunt morels out the window. "It's pretty much a crap shoot anyway," Bob says, "but it's near impossible to guess right this year when the little bit of predictability in the sport has been taken away by the drought."

Now, here came two more folks—both guys in denim bibs and McGregor baseball caps looking a lot like Tweedledum and Tweedledee—which seemed appropriate given that this breakfast was turning into an *Alice in Wonderland* kind of experience. Turns out they were bachelor brothers named Paul and Pomeroy ("Pom" for short) who farm together just up the road and eat breakfast and dinner at the Long Branch most every day. Bob introduced us all around and explained that we were looking to go morel hunting but didn't know "nuthin" about it so the group was assembled to help us out. Pom said that Joe, another farmer "down the way," is a big morel hunter—"don't like to eat 'em but loves to hunt 'em." He says that Joe was finding them "down low" a week or so ago but now is finding them "up high." That seemed to settle it for everybody but Summer and me.

Now Bob and Bonnie and Paul were all agreeing that we should go "up high" which apparently meant we were going beyond Jubilee Lake to find an old logging road that's not very well maintained but "probably passable," at least in most places. Pat came back with my glasses and I actually could see a little better with them, so everybody gathered around looking for the turn off to Jubilee Lake again so they could show me how to get there.

I overheard Summer telling Miss Mae about her boyfriend's family and how they recently moved from Columbus, Ohio to Lubbock, Texas where his dad had taken a new job. Miss Mae said she has a brother in Texas who's gotten hard of hearing so she doesn't call him anymore and only writes him occasionally because he never writes her back. Rose was telling

Miss Mae that Summer couldn't care less about her brother and saying, "Ain't that right?" to Summer who was looking my way hoping for a sign that we needed to be moving on. That's when Bonnie saved the day saying we'd better get going if we were going to find any morels and that she'd meet me at the cash register. Pat then handed me Bob's map saying Bob "don't need it" and looking at Bob like he'd better not put up a fight.

Bottom line: I didn't get to eat any breakfast or drink my coffee and Summer pretty much ended up in the same boat; but we did get an introduction to a new sport and were headed off on a new dad/daughter adventure with Bob's unreadable map in hand and some vague idea about what we were doing in our heads.

As we exited the Long Branch, Bonnie yelled after us saying that we might want to stop by The Chalet up at Tollgate and check in with them just to see if they had any ideas for us. So we jumped in the rig and trucked out of Weston headed for the top of the mountains. We drove up, up, up through mountain meadows full of blue and orange wildflowers.

Summer and I were still hungry, having not eaten much at our breakfast stop. So we figured a quick snack break at The Chalet was a pretty good idea even if we couldn't get any additional morel hunting advice. A half hour later we saw The Chalet off on the left and pulled into the empty parking lot next to what looked like an abandoned hotel/restaurant with a neon "Open" sign lit up in the window. Summer and I wandered into the restaurant wondering where the people were when Rita appeared from the back asking what she could do for us.

We sat at the bar and ordered a cup of coffee and a couple of pieces of strawberry rhubarb pie—probably the last of the season, Rita said. While Rita cut our pie slices, Summer mentioned that we were coming up to go fishing but had switched our plan to morel hunting after encouragement from some folks down in Weston. Summer, who can be very tactful and occasionally clever, then said that those Weston folks told us to stop at The Chalet and ask for advice because they thought folks at The Chalet would know most everything about the current state of morel hunting "up high."

Well, those few words had the desired effect. Rita started in on the long history of morel hunting in The Blues and how she and her twin sisters had been raised on morels mixed in with scrambled eggs— which she still thinks is the best way to eat them. Her mom's favorite way to fix them is just to sauté them in butter with a little salt and pepper and serve them alongside chicken fried steak and gravy.

About that time we heard the doorbell jingle and here came a guy who Rita greeted as Micah but who looked a lot like Methuselah—or at least what I think Methuselah would look like. He set himself down at the bar next to me. Without any exchange of words between them, Rita popped the top on a 16oz Bud Light and placed it in front of Micah while she continued her soliloquy on the local lore of morel hunting.

Micah drank his beer and fingered the two packs of unfiltered Camels in his shirt pocket but didn't say a word while Rita moved her lesson from recipes to identification and collection. She had a big pot full of morels soaking in salt water back in the kitchen, which she retrieved and set on the counter between Summer and me. Well, this sort of grabbed Micah's attention and he leaned over to see the huge "blondes" and "blacks" that filled the pot. He fished around in the pot looking to see if there were any "calf brains" in there while telling us that they should be appearing about now alongside the morels; that some folks won't eat 'em for fear of getting sick; but he's eaten 'em all his life and loves 'em.

Well, that big pot of mushrooms was just what we needed to get Micah to open up and engage Rita in a debate on where that pot of mushrooms had come from, " 'cause they was picked by Arnold and brought in for me and my husband but he didn't tell me where he got 'em—nobody ever does," according to Rita.

Micah offered that he had been hunting "down low" but that the mushrooms "down there" had started to get soft and wormy so he'd hunted "up high" yesterday afternoon near "where the pavement ends up the Lake road." He'd found a few but hadn't done as well as he'd hoped. Summer was saying to Rita that the Weston folks had directed us to the high meadows above Jubilee Lake but neither Rita nor Micah thought we needed to go all that way to hunt.

Rita went off to the store room to get us a potato sack saying that whatever we collected we should put in a mesh type bag so the spores could fall out of the collected morels while we hunted for more. Micah said we shouldn't pick anything "smaller than your fat thumb" while he drew a map on the back of a napkin for us.

Long story short: We said our thanks, paid our bill, bought Micah another tall one and headed out the door. We drove up to the area Micah had directed us to and hunted for several hours without seeing another human—our only company being a cool wind blowing in under the pine trees where we found about three dozen big fat firm blondes and a few blacks before deciding that we needed to find a lunch spot and then drive on back to the farm.

We had a great time. Summer really got into the hunting and did a much better job of spotting the elusive morels than I did. I mostly found every type of mushroom other than morels and spent my time trying to guess which ones would cause death after inflicting severe intestinal distress followed by paralysis and slow suffocation.

That night I cut the morels lengthwise and soaked them in cold salt water for about 15 minutes to drive the bugs out. After drying them off, Summer helped me sauté them in butter until fully cooked but still firm. Annie grated some fresh Parmesan cheese, which we sprinkled over the morels along with some salt and a little fresh ground black pepper.

Summer dumped the morels onto a big plate while

I opened a bottle of Yellowhawk Cellars Muscat. We retired to the porch, sat under the slowly revolving ceiling fans, and settled in to eat our morels—just picking them off the plate with our fingers—savoring our wine and boring Annie with our day's stories. The mushrooms were fabulous—earthy fragrance, a little smoky in flavor, and all the better because they followed a day full of morel hunting adventure.

So, put next May on your calendar for a trip over here to hunt morels and tell Scott we say "hi." And please don't tell him what I said about his not having a "good side" to photograph.

Best,
SAM

Family Matters

Dear Steve:

I don't know if you'll remember it but you told me when I was writing my first book that I needed to be sensitive to the "family thing." You told me that, no matter how much a person might beg, I should not let any family member read the book before it was printed and cast in stone.

Well, I mostly took your advice. I didn't tell anybody I was writing a book, except Annie. I told her that I was not letting her read it because it was a 30th wedding anniversary present and I wanted it to be a surprise. I also told her it was a secret from the rest of the world, too, because I didn't know whether there ever would really be a book and didn't want folks asking me everyday for the rest of my life when I was going to finish the thing.

Well, I now know that you are a very wise and good friend. You said that no matter what I wrote, or how I named the characters, or how much I sugarcoated the truth, relations would work hard to parse the words and find things to be sensitive to and get irritated about. In addition, I am now finding that Annie's friends are reading the book and helping her analyze me as a flawed and only moderately interesting human being. As a result of all this, I am learning a lot of stuff about my family and myself I didn't know. I figured you might find this interesting.

By and large, Annie seems to be happy with her character in the book mostly because her daughters and friends are telling her that she came off pretty good. The whole time I was writing the book and not letting her preview it, you could see her stewing about what I might say about her or our kids or her family.

She thinks I can be a little insensitive and lack the emotional intelligence to see where I am stepping on the feelings of other people. While she was excited to see what I was going to write because it would give her a better view into the real person hiding inside my inscrutable exterior, she was also a little afraid because she wasn't in a position to "fix" the parts of the book that would undoubtedly need her editing. In short, not being able to read my drafts drove her nuts.

One day last November, I printed out the first few chapters so I could edit them by hand and inadvertently left those pages lying on the living room table with my computer and research books while I went to get the oil changed in the truck. When I got back, there was Annie sitting in her chair reading as fast as she could. I played hell getting her to give up those papers; she kept saying she'd almost read all of what I'd left on the table and I might as well let her finish it. Well, I was having none of that and told her that she was ruining the surprise. She whimpered and pleaded but I took those pages back and put them away. She said that it was my fault for leaving the pages out where she couldn't help but see them and that I needed to be more careful about hiding my writing.

Then she launched in on how the first story in the book needed to be "revised" because . . . well, you get the point. I told Annie that she was acting out the best reason I knew for not letting her read the book in advance and that my book didn't need her to fix it.

Now, Annie is not known for her secret-keeping ability but she did a pretty good job of managing her spill-the-beans tendencies until near the end. Believe it or not, I was almost finished with the book before Annie couldn't hold the secret any longer and started telling everybody within earshot.

At first it was, "Well, I've only told the kids; you can't write a book and not tell your own children; they'd be hurt that you felt you couldn't trust them with the secret."

Then it was, "Well, I've only told my mom and my sister and they're way back in Virginia and won't tell anybody."

When her brother called and asked me when we were sending them a copy of the book, she said, "Well it's only Buck; you can't expect mom to keep the secret from the family."

And then, just three day later, Ellen, the lady who cuts my hair here in Walla Walla says, "Hey Sam, I hear you wrote a book."

Annie still wonders why I don't tell her everything.

When the book came out, Jolie showed up out here

at the farm, got her copy, jumped back into her car and disappeared. Her friend, Hannah, told me a few days later that Jolie had gone straight to her room with book in hand and flipped through the entire text—back to front—looking for every mention of her name and reading those paragraphs to see what I was saying about her. After she'd completed her examination, she called and asked me if she could get ten copies to hand out to her friends. So, I'm guessing that she felt okay about her character and her role in the book, but I'm still unclear on whether she's ever read the whole thing.

Summer was in Honduras when the books arrived, so it took a couple of weeks for her to get her copy. In the interim, Annie, Marshall and Jolie reported to Summer via email on her parts in the book. I've heard, through Annie, that after Summer read the book, she was basically happy with what I said about her but would like for me to emphasize her intelligence, creativity and daring nature in the next book.

Marshall says she read the whole book, cover to cover, in one sitting and came away from the experience much relieved.

So, now several of Annie's friends have read the book at her request and are reporting on their analysis of me and the state of my psyche as it relates to our marital relationship.

Thankfully, they are telling her that her husband's affection for her came through loud and clear and this has got Annie all puffed up with satisfaction. Linda told Annie she thought that there were a few too many references to Annie's inquisitive side and Mary told her that the book suggested she had a tendency to stick her nose in where it didn't need to be. But both of them thought that, on balance, the book was a very positive review of her as a person. So, whew! I dodged a bullet on that one.

Annie's friends are also telling her that while I am a flawed and only moderately interesting human being, I am mostly a normal male and probably a little better than some they've known, so Annie is now thinking that maybe I'm not so bad after all. I guess that was the best outcome I could have hoped for.

Anyway, I just thought you might find my actual experience with the "family thing" of interest. Please give Joanne our best. We miss seeing you guys. Write when you can.

Best,
SAM

Gone Fishing . . . Again

Dear John:

I'm sorry that our fishing trip didn't work out. I was looking forward to it. I know that work can get in the way of things. Maybe we can hook up in the fall and go steelhead fishing like we talked about.

Anyway, turns out I managed to go on without you. I haven't yet found a fishing buddy here locally, so Annie agreed to go with me and we just struck off on our own for a small stream that Mike, our Forest Service friend, told me about. I can't tell you where it is mostly because I'm not quite sure myself but I can tell you that it is as pretty a spot as I've ever seen on this planet.

From here at the farm you drive about two hours on barely passable mountain roads until you run into a Forest Service gate blocking further vehicular progress. That's where you put on your hiking boots and walk another couple of miles along an abandoned homestead road until you come up on the stream. It runs for about half a mile down through a big, open meadow and disappears into the trees below the meadow.

When we were there, the wildflowers were out in full bloom. There were so many little purple flowers blooming that the meadow looked like a 50-acre bedspread rippling in the wind. It was just the two of us out in the woods on an 80° gorgeous day, up on top of the world, standing under blue skies and cotton ball fluffy clouds, with snow-covered peaks all around.

Annie and I dropped our backpacks, spread out an old quilt on the ground by the stream, and started to pull on our waders. It was while we were rigging our fly rods that Annie noticed an old bull elk strolling across the lower end of the meadow. He stopped once to chew some grass and give us the once over, but I guess we didn't rate much of a look because he just ambled on downstream and disappeared into the woods. The only other living creatures in evidence were two handfuls of tiny yellow birds that Annie identified as some type of swallow.

As we went down to the water, I reached down to move an old tree limb and spied morel mushrooms growing amongst the weeds. Annie then saw a few more just a couple of feet from the first ones. And I saw a few more along the upstream bank. Well, that pretty much killed our focus on fishing and Annie went back up to our makeshift picnic site to get some mesh bags out of her backpack. Thankfully she'd brought several to put wet clothes in—just in case.

For the next hour we wandered down the stream bank in our fishing garb, poking our way along under the overhanging cottonwoods and tamarack, and collected morels until we were quite sure we couldn't think of another person we could give some to. I just love morels sautéed in butter and Annie likes this creamy morel pasta dish we make when we can get a big batch of the fresh mushrooms.

The wind started to kick up a bit and I noticed a hatch of mayflies coming off the water. As soon as those bugs appeared, there were beautiful native Red Band trout rising everywhere—water ringlets arcing out from fish noses breaking the surface. Annie and I got back on track, tied on tiny little dry flies, and crawled back down to the stream, maintaining a very low profile. On her second cast, Annie hooked into a good fish and fought him for a few minutes before landing him and releasing him back into the frigid water.

While she was releasing her fish, I noticed a huge fish's head appearing and disappearing with cadence-like regularity just beyond a log near the far bank. The log that hid this lunker lay in the stream in such a way as to divert water into a small side channel that veered well away from the main stream into some tall brush. Annie encouraged me to go take a shot at what she was now calling the "mother of all trout." To get a decent cast into that little side channel I had to wade waist deep across the stream, climb in under a stream-side willow stand and crouch down into a little puddle of dead water left over from the spring snowmelt. I had just managed to get into position to cast when I noticed that there were literally hundreds of mosquitoes hovering around my head and landing on every little bit of my exposed flesh.

The choice was to swat mosquitoes and spook the fish, or offer myself up as a pincushion and concentrate on making a good cast. I chose the latter and managed a decent downstream cast while flipping extra line out the rod tip to insure a good drag-free fly float down to the fish that was still feeding easily in the very slow current. I watched patiently as my fly inched its way down the thread of that tiny side stream. Annie whispered encouragement from her vantage point. As quietly as you please, that big old head bulged back to the surface and sipped my fly down. And that's when all hell broke loose.

I don't know what I was thinking and, in retrospect, I realize that I was not thinking—at least not very well. As I moved from squatting to standing and raised my rod tip to set the hook, that big Red Band went straight up into the air and Annie started dancing up and down bank like a nest of ants had crawled in her waders. She was way more excited than I was—mostly because she'd seen that big guy go airborne and I'd only glimpsed his acrobatics through the maze of willow branches that surrounded me. Once standing, I came to understand my next problem—how to get myself, my fly rod and several feet of fly line out of the willows without losing what was, based on the quality of Annie's whooping and jumping, probably one of the nicest fish I'd ever tempted to one of my flies.

Well, I'm quite sure you don't care how I extricated myself from the mess I was in, but I have to tell you that I didn't come fully free until I'd managed to fall backwards into the stream and fill my waders with water so cold it'd make your toes curl. I came up spluttering and Annie commenced laughing so hard she couldn't breathe. Now my entire backside was wet and muddy from head to toe and my teeth were starting to chatter from the cold, but I was free of that willow stand and, remarkably, the big one was still on my line.

Without thinking through the possible outcomes (which had already proven perilous), I began to move up into that tiny side channel believing that the fish, like most fish, would move further away from me and deeper into the willows that appeared to swallow up that little bit of water.

Once again, the unexpected came at me full throttle. Instead of running down that channel away from me and probably breaking my fly line in the process, that big fish came straight at me—headed for the safety of the fast running main stream that was now behind me. As I frantically tried to take up line, he went straight between my feet and headed for the bank where Annie was still doing her little dance.

So I did what anyone would have done, I raised my leg and started turning around so as to get my fly line out from between my legs and face the fish who was also now behind me and moving away with speed.

Now, what would you guess I saw as I turned to look back for that fish and Annie? Here comes a young couple—both buck naked except for hiking boots—and they stroll up beside Annie as if nothing were amiss. I'd give a lot of money for a picture of Annie's face as she looked those young people from head to crotch taking in their nakedness and then looking back at me, tears still streaming from her eyes—the remnants of her laughing fit.

Well, here came my next mistake. Instead of concentrating on my feet and where they needed to go to keep up with my trophy fish, I found myself staring bug-eyed along with Annie at our visitors. And then I went down again—a perfect face plant into that fast moving current.

It seemed like an eternity passed before I managed to get my head back above water, the rest of me still submerged with my waders now completely full of water. I don't know how he moved so quickly, but Naked Guy was suddenly there beside me, and hauling me up, with my wife and her new (and gorgeous, I might add) naked friend applauding Naked Guy's heroics.

So here I am standing in the middle of a picture perfect little trout stream with a naked guy holding me upright when I realize that I'm still holding my fly rod and, miracle of miracles, that big fish is still on. So I turn to fight my fish, oblivious to the fact that my whole body is turning blue from the cold. Surprisingly, Naked Guy (we still have not been properly introduced) is still standing right beside me in that water and cheering—seemingly okay with the fact that he is waist deep in frigid ice melt. I yelled to Annie that I needed her landing net, so Naked Girl helped Annie unhook the net while Naked Guy waded back to the stream bank to retrieve it.

Long story short, I did land that fish. Naked Guy and I measured him against the markings on my fly rod and figured his length at roughly 24 inches—a very big trout in anybody's book.

Back on shore I couldn't wait to pull off my waders and managed to spill several gallons of liquid ice on the ground around me while thanking our new naked friends for the timely rescue and assistance. Naked Guy introduced himself as Brad and his voluptuous friend as Nina.

After everybody said "hi" all around, Annie blurted out the "Where are your clothes?" question. Nothing like getting straight to the heart of the matter.

Nina explained that they were naturists and often camped in the area because they never saw anybody else. Today, however, they'd heard all the commotion and Annie's howls of laughter and had donned their hiking boots to walk down our way and see what was going on. Well, we could have just thanked them again and let them go with a few goodbye pleasantries, but Annie was having none of that; her curiosity was now piqued to the point of at least twenty questions on the difference between naturists and naturalists and the advisability of walking buck naked through fields filled with prickly things and blood-sucking insects.

Finally I suggested to Annie (who now seemed surprisingly comfortable around naked people) that Nina and Brad probably had something better to do than stand around gabbing with us when we needed to be thinking about getting Sam into some dry clothes, and that broke up the party. The naked folks wandered back to their well hidden campsite and we struck out for the car—two miles up the path—with wet waders and bags full of morels slung over our shoulders. I should add that we offered Brad and Nina one of those big bags of morels but they allowed as how they'd already eaten their fill every meal for the last two days.

Now it will not surprise you that Annie's encounter with in-your-face nudity had her brain spinning questions faster than we could cover them. It was interesting that Annie has now lived a life spanning more than a half-century but was, until that day, unaware of the withering effects of extreme cold on the male anatomy. I am guessing that she had studied Naked Guy before and after he rescued me and had been shocked at the immediate and dramatic anatomical change Naked Guy had suffered at the hands of that ice-cold water. She wanted to know if only cold water "worked." "What about cold air?" "Does it hurt?" And on and on . . .

So, if you've got a better story than that, don't waste your time writing it down because, I can already tell you, nobody will believe it. Annie says she only believes this fish story because she was there. And she says to tell Marilyn we say "hey."

Best,
SAM

Making Cheese

D ear Steve:

We got your letter and are happy to hear that your big neighborhood party went so well. Annie and I are sorry that we couldn't make it back to Seattle that weekend. And yes, the cheese you bought at the local farmers' market from the Monteillet Fromagerie is the cheese I was telling you about. I'm glad everybody enjoyed it.

Joan and Pierre-Louis do a real nice job. Annie and I regularly go up to Dayton to see them and buy more cheese. It's about a 45-minute drive from the farm but the trip up through the rolling wheat fields is pretty nice. Annie loves to go and play with the baby goats and lambs. And I like sampling whatever Joan has out on her cheese board.

The fromagerie undergoes constant expansion because the demand for Joan and Pierre-Louis' cheeses has been growing faster than anybody can imagine. But no matter how busy things get around the place, Joan and Pierre-Louis always seem to have time to sit out under the grape arbor and drink a glass of wine with us. It is a nice spot—great views out across the pastures where sheep graze and goats forage, beautiful big white Pyrenees dogs watch over their flocks, and chickens squabble with one another. There are comfortable chairs in the shade under the grape vines, a nice breeze coming up the valley between the hills, and plenty of cheeses to sample. It doesn't get much better than this.

It has been a real joy getting to know this couple. They've been a big help to us as we've thought about what we're going to do on the farm. We first met Joan and Pierre-Louis as we started looking for some land to buy. Annie was thinking about raising goats, milking them and handing the milk off to me so I could make cheeses. Well, watching the Monteillets—up at dawn, working until it's too dark to see, eating dinner late, and going to bed well after Annie's normal bedtime—soon convinced us that cheese-making was not our thing. As farm life has evolved for us, Annie has bought a couple of pet goats from Joan—the ones we call Bobo and Snacks—and they have livened things up out in the pastures. But that's as far as we've gone with goats. Annie's now thinking about breeding Bobo and milking her after her baby arrives next spring so we can make cottage cheese and a few cheeses to age— to supplement what we buy from Joan and Pierre-Louis.

Anyway, I think you'll get a kick out of their story. It is a storybook kind of romance. Somebody'll probably be doing the movie one of these days. I won't do it justice, but here goes:

Pierre-Louis Monteillet was born in the south of France in the small village of Millau—just twenty miles from the town of Roquefort—yep, the place where they make the famous Roquefort sheep milk cheeses that are aged in the limestone caves of the region.

In Millau, sheep hides are processed into finely tanned leather and made into clothing—particularly the famous Millau leather gloves. As a very young boy, Pierre-Louis sat with his mother and his aunts while they hand-sewed the glove patterns into the leather. It was work that allowed mothers to be home with their children and visit with family and neighbors.

Pierre-Louis' family ran a small café in Millau. One of Pierre-Louis' jobs each day was to run across the street to see Felix, the neighborhood baker, and pick up the fresh croissants that would be sold with small cups of dark coffee in the morning, and with jambon and local sheep cheeses—like the delicious soft-ripened Perail—in the afternoon. When he was old enough, Pierre-Louis worked in the wheat fields with the men—helping to harvest the wheat that would produce those wonderful croissants, and catching field mice, which he kept in his pocket as companions while he worked.

There are hundreds of limestone caves in the vicinity of Millau. As a young boy, Pierre-Louis explored those caves and became quite a good spelunker. He also developed a bad case of wanderlust. Every chance he got, he'd take off with friends—traveling the Mediterranean and exploring caves from France to Turkey to Morocco. Soon, his world expanded into Africa where he explored caves and culture—at one point traveling with a goatherd across the Sahara to visit the Tuareg people where he milked the goats to help out with the chores.

By 1975, Pierre-Louis had finished his schooling, worked for a few years, and saved up enough money to take off on his biggest travel adventure. He spent the next three years wandering the world—hitchhiking through Europe, Africa, and South America; staying in hostels and eating just enough to get by.

Sometime in early 1978, he found his way to Quebec where he hooked up with his friend Michel, and they struck out for Mexico to see the Aztecan ruins and live among the locals; they ended up in Oaxaca where Michel developed a bad case of Montezuma's Revenge and took to his youth hostel bed—down the hall from the communal bathroom.

Now, unbeknownst to Pierre-Louis, his future bride was staying in the same hostel—just down the hall . . . but I digress . . .

"Kathy" was a tomboy—as near as she could get to being a son to her doting father. Her parents were wheat farmers just outside Walla Walla and "Kathy" was a farm girl. She was independent, strong-willed, strikingly beautiful, and handy around a combine. She could run like the wind and ride like a rodeo cowgirl. In high school, she was a track team star, a barrel racing legend and a fixture on the sports page.

(Pierre-Louis will show you the scrapbook full of "Kathy's" pictures if Joan won't.)

"Kathy" married young—during her college years—and divorced young. She has no regrets; she says "whatever doesn't kill you makes you stronger" and tends to see the bright side of almost every part of her life. She returned to Walla Walla and became a chef in a Main Street restaurant. And during the slow cold winter months of 1978, "Kathy" decided she needed to take a trip—preferably to a warm, sunny place. So, she struck out with a friend of hers for . . . you guessed it . . . Oaxaca, Mexico where she—now traveling as "Leena"—and her friend found a room *with a private bathroom* at a local hostel.

Now, back to the romantic part: "Leena" looked out her hostel window one day to see Michel running down the narrow street, white as a sheet, dripping with sweat. The next thing she heard was somebody swearing in French and pounding on the bathroom door down the hall. She opened her room door and there she saw Michel—desperately trying to get into the communal bathroom—so she offered her private bathroom, which Michel occupied for quite some time while "Leena" waited patiently in the hall. (By the way, that is not the romantic part; it's coming up.)

When Michel emerged, looking much relieved, he thanked her, introduced himself, explained his digestive system distress, and begged "Leena" to join him, *and a friend of his*, for dinner that night followed by a bit of late-night bar hopping and dancing. For a guy with Montezuma's Revenge, he didn't let much get in the way of a good time. "Leena" equivocated but didn't say no, and watched Michel retreat to his bed down the hall.

"Leena" went back to her seat at the window and watched the local women in their brightly colored clothes chatting in the street. And that's when she spied another guy strolling unhurriedly down the street toward the hostel. (This is the romantic part.) He was lean and tan with long dark hair, looking very "exotic" according to "Leena." She watched as he entered the front door of the hostel below her window; she heard him mounting the stairs and went to out into the hallway in time to see the "exotic" man enter Michel's room at the end of the hall. And that's when she ran down the hall, rapped politely on Michel's door, and introduced herself as "Leena" to the exotic man, who introduced himself as (you guessed it) Pierre-Louis. And that's when "Leena" told Michel that she was free for dinner after all.

"Leena" spent the rest of the afternoon shopping and blew all of her remaining cash on one of those brightly colored Oaxacan outfits. Then she went back to the hostel, changed into her new clothes, and strolled down the hall to find Pierre-Louis and Michel.

They went to dinner; they went dancing; they drank a few local beers; and they went swimming in the fountain at 3:00am. They spent the next several days together. "Leena" says Pierre-Louis was smitten; but my guess is that "smitten" was a two-way street.

Soon it was time for "Leena" to return to Walla Walla and her chef's job. Pierre-Louis was headed south with Michel. So they reluctantly said their goodbyes, parted company, and went on with their separate lives.

(Now, this is not a good place to stop this kind of story. It is, however, the kind of place that a TV producer would pick to stop, cut to several minutes of commercials, and then say "To Be Continued" after you'd waited patiently to see the conclusion. Thankfully, I'm not that cruel.)

A week or two passed. "Leena" was back in Walla Walla and had returned to life as "Kathy." Pierre-Louis was but a memory. "Kathy" told her friends stories about him but pretty much figured that he'd only been an incident in her life—a nice one.

And that's when "Kathy's" roommate came rushing into the restaurant one night and ran into the kitchen to find "Kathy" and tell her that a fellow named Pierre-Louis was in town at her house looking for the captivating "Leena"—that he'd hitchhiked from Mexico to Walla Walla with only a scrap of paper in his pocket bearing "Leena's" address.

You can guess at the rest of the story but I'll tell it to you anyway. Captivating "Kathy" ripped off her apron, threw it at her assistant, told him to "take over" and ran like the wind (I told you she could run like the wind) back to her house and into the arms of her exotic Pierre-Louis.

They traveled together; they visited Pierre-Louis's family in France; they returned to Walla Walla, married and took over management of Joan's family wheat farm—just the two of them—miles from the nearest neighbors.

For almost twenty years they farmed together—working from sun up to well after sundown, ten months of the year. In the other two months, they traveled—often to Pierre-Louis' little French village where they lived among his relatives, got interested in raising animals and learned about cheese-making. By 1996, they had settled on their dream—to build a fromagerie. They bought land just west of Dayton, fixed up the house that came with the property and started making plans for their new life.

Just five years ago, Joan and Pierre-Louis bought their first milking goats and sheep, and started making cheese. Today, they own 23 sheep and 27 goats; they make about 500 pounds of fresh and aged cheeses each week during the milking season; and they ship their award-winning cheeses all over the US and sell through farmers' markets in Seattle and Portland. It has not been easy; they work hard; they're very busy people; and they're living their dream every day.

But no matter how busy they are, they're never too busy to see you and show you what they're doing. They may put you to work while you're visiting with them, but they won't rush you off. Before you know it, you've sampled five or six of their cheeses, drunk a couple of glasses of wine, seen Joan's latest glass art project (yep, I forgot to tell you that Joan is quite an artist), and bought several rounds of cheese, a couple of pounds of butter and a dozen free-range duck eggs. It's a nice way to pass the time.

So, the next time you're here, we're going to take a little trip to Dayton. Feel free to ask Joan why she's got so many aliases. She won't give you a straight answer but whatever she tells you will be interesting. And ask Pierre-Louis about the lovely Nelly; there's a good story there somewhere.

Best,
SAM

Mowing the Grass

Dear Peter:

Thanks for your letter. I am sort of looking forward to hearing about your trip to Africa. It is unfortunate that your camera broke in a place where there was no hope of getting it repaired. I'm sure you can't imagine what happened to it, but I can. I'm guessing that it died of overuse.

Annie is sitting here saying that I should be nice. She says that one way or the other you are going to get us into a place where we won't be able to escape and you are going to make us look at several thousand of your pictures whether we like it or not. She thinks we will save ourselves a lot of heartache if we just submit and try to enjoy it. So, in the spirit of developing a positive attitude about what is coming anyway, I want to invite you to bring the best one thousand of your pictures when you come out here next month and tell you how much we are looking forward to looking at each of them. I'll lay in a good store of our friend Douglas' coffee to make sure that Annie doesn't nod off during your fascinating travelogue. Does Peggy know that she's going to have to endure it again?

To answer your question, yes I did get the tractor. It is a 1978 JD 4240, so it's pretty old—27 years old to be exact—but it only has 5000 hours on it and is in surprisingly good shape. A couple of our neighbors looked it over for me and said, "she'll do," so we bought it and got it trucked over here where Tom fired "her" up and parked her in the shed. She packs about 100 horsepower, which should be more than plenty for anything we'll want to do around the farm.

It was several days before I got up the nerve to climb up in the cab and take her for a spin. I read the operator's manual before I climbed aboard but once I got into the driver's seat all that book learning went out the window. I didn't have any implements yet so all I could do was ride her up and down the drive-way—pulling on levers to see if they'd do anything. Some did and some didn't.

Well, Annie just laughs at me but I have to say that there is something very satisfying about sitting up on top of that big powerhouse and listening to her diesel engine rumble as we chug along. I had a feeling that I was finally armed with the firepower I needed to do stuff on 160 acres that I simply couldn't do with our 22-inch self-propelled push mower or a wheelbarrow and shovel.

It took a few weeks, but Tom finally found a used Bush Hog Legend—a big, honking mower that cuts about a 12-foot swath and eagerly shreds almost any-thing that gets in the way—grass, small trees, old irri-gation pipe, and ancient fence posts long since taken

out of commission and left hidden deep in the tall weeds.

I'll have to write you another letter on dealing with weeds. I have learned way more about this important subject than I'd ever hoped to know. Suffice to say that there are three ways to deal with invasive weeds that want to turn your grassy meadow into a landowner's nightmare: "spray 'em, mow 'em or ignore 'em."

I am not willing to ignore them and the Local Weed Control Board wouldn't let me if I were.

By mowing, you hope to keep the weeds from seeding out and propagating their onslaught. There are lots of plusses and minuses to mowing that I won't bore you with here. The bottom line is that I decided to take a shot at mowing to control weeds and maintain a decent firebreak around the farmhouse and barn, so the next grass fire out our way doesn't take down in ten minutes what we spent about a year putting up.

Anyway, Tom helped me get the mower hooked up and the two of us climbed up into the tractor cab together so he could show me how to play with the levers to get power to the mower, set the mowing height, and raise and lower the mower wings (yep, wings that raise up to get through gates and tight places and then lower down to wreak their havoc). He rode with me as we took one mowing pass around the perimeter of the meadow and then essentially said he'd had enough of sitting in my lap; he'd taught me the basics, and figured that I could learn the nuances of heavy-duty mowing without him.

So there I was, alone on the land, sitting on top of 100 horses, pulling a ton of mowing fury behind me. The first hour or so was a little nerve wracking but pretty soon I fell into the rhythm of it and started to see what was going on around me out there. It will not surprise you that field mice and other small rodents feel somewhat threatened by big equipment bearing down on them. So, they run—generally off to the left or right of the nose of the tractor. Well, the hawks out our way are pretty savvy hunters and are always looking for an easy meal. They have learned that big equipment moving across open pastureland lays a delicious-looking smorgasbord of small animal treats.

Four or five hawks flew in from their regular haunts and hovered above me over the tractor like they were suspended up there. When they'd see one of those tasty little morsels run for its life, they'd drop out of the sky like falling rock, grab a squirming mouthful in their claws and beat their wings furiously to get out of my way before becoming a test of the mower's ability to de-bone raptors. Those guys would take their meals off to a high branch in one of the trees along the river, wolf them down, and be ready for the next dining opportunity by the time I had completed another pass around the property.

By the time I'd logged my fourth hour of mowing and had lapsed into complete boredom, it occurred to me that I'd had the same sort of experience somewhere else; and then it dawned on me that pasture mowing is a lot like open sea sailing. You sit on a cushioned seat with your hand loosely on the wheel; you constantly watch the trim of your sails without really noticing that you're noticing; you spend a lot of time daydreaming or admiring the sea around you; and then you start wondering how much longer you have to do it.

I decided to head back into port. The rest of that pasture would wait for its mowing—at least until tomorrow.

So that was it—my version of Intro to Mowing

101. Since then I've spent at least another 40 hours perched on top of my John Deere, cruising the land— sometimes seeing things I'd never noticed before, but mostly just letting my mind drift wherever it wanted to go. I'll have to say that I've really gotten into it and look forward to late summer when I'll get to mowing again.

I'm reluctant to tell anybody around here how much I like riding the range; I'm guessing some of the neighbors would be pretty happy to put me on their tractors and let me have all the fun.

Can't wait to see your pictures . . .

Best,
SAM

Graduation

Dear Coco:

Your friend was right and I was wrong. The wind does occasionally blow like a banshee out here on the prairie. I had thought the big winds were reserved for the wind farms stretching across the Horse Heaven Hills to our south. But occasionally some of that big wind does spill off those slopes and find its way to the floor of the valley where we live. Spring seems to be the best time to watch one of these windstorms roll across The Land carrying truckloads of dust and cart-wheeling tumbleweeds across the meadow.

After I get over the initial shock and awe of one of these storms and remind myself that Greg, the builder, did do an admirable job of fastening our house to the dirt, I can settle into a chair out on the porch and watch the show—and it is quite a show. These fast moving storms remind me a lot of the afternoon squalls we survived on family trips to the beach when the kids were little.

Anyway, the big Whitman College graduation came

off without a hitch and Jolie managed to walk away with her diploma. She got her degree and we got a massive dose of financial relief. It was a good day. Sorry it has taken me so long to write to tell you about it.

The party out at the farm on Friday night before graduation was a huge success—and I do mean "huge." Jolie was graduating with twenty-five of her closest female friends, so they all got together and organized a shindig for themselves, their families and male admirers. I was not invited to participate in the planning, so I really had no idea until that night what the girls and their moms had cooked up. Annie sent me away on Friday morning to "go write something" while they set up for the crowd. "Well," I said, "is there anything I can help with?" And Annie said, "Nope. We're on top of it. Just show up back here at the house at 6:00pm and prepare yourself to be pleasant"—which I mostly am anyway.

So, I did—show up at 6:00pm that is. You haven't seen the house, barn, and cottage yet but there is an open area in the middle of those buildings just right for a party tent, dance floor, dinner tables and a buffet dinner line. The kids managed to find room for a several kegs of beer and the moms leaned on their winemaker friends for a few cases of wine. They'd gotten the Worm Ranch to cater dinner and the cooks were there in force a little before the magic hour to set up all the food. The graduates had also arranged a bus to cart folks from town out to the farm and back so the imbibing partygoers could drink a few beers and leave the driving to someone else.

By 6:30pm two bus loads had been dropped off and there were 250 people—ages 2 to 91—lined up for one of the best Mexican food dinners anybody had ever eaten—homemade tamales, quesadillas, jalapeño poppers, enchiladas, and burritos drizzled with a spicy green tomatillo sauce—all fresh and filling. Plates were piled high and the beer ran freely. The Worm Ranch did a really nice job.

The Rogues, a local trio, played Irish ballads, country and bluegrass, and folks danced in pairs until Jerry, a graduate's dad, offered to call "a few square dances." And he did . . . for the next three hours.

Annie spent much of the night showing the animal lovers her alpacas and the rest of the menagerie. Bobo, our little female goat, bleated, the alpacas hummed and the dogs barked at, or to, the music.

It can get a little chilly around here as the sun disappears in the evening; there's not much atmospheric moisture to hold the heat of the day. By sundown, parents and grandparents had left the dance floor to the kids and parked themselves around a big bonfire out in the field below the barn or on the front porch of the house in front of the fireplace out there. Everybody seemed to be having a good time.

I enjoyed it all but was frankly pretty happy to see the last bus depart about 11:00pm.

On Saturday morning, I signed books at the Farmers' Market with Jeffrey (who'd done the cover art for the book). We chatted with neighbors and Jeffrey introduced me to some local folks I hadn't met. Bob from The Oddfellows Home wanted to know if we could come and talk with their older residents about writing the book and getting it published. Ray and Imelda from Florida stopped to ask about our move to Walla Walla. Their daughter, Amy, had taken a job at Whitman College and they were interested in knowing how she was going to find the transition. Peggy, who'd bought the book at Merchants Delicatessen up the street, showed up to get the book signed for her parents who now reside in Naples, Florida. And that led to a very long discussion with Ray and Imelda in front of our booth about Florida and humidity, and Walla Walla and heat, and on and on, while other folks waited patiently. Seemed like most of the people in line were eating pastries and drinking coffee, so I'm not sure they were in any hurry anyway.

The Walla Walla Farmers' Market has become quite a big deal around here—fresh produce, nursery stock, snacks of all types (including Walla Walla Sweet Onion sausages on a bun), artwork, crafts, goat milk soaps, onion this and that in little jars, jams, jellies, homemade pies and cakes, the best tabouli I've ever eaten, clothing made out of local wools and alpaca fiber, and just about anything else you'd expect to see. The Rogues had gotten up early after our Friday night bash and were back at it, playing on the market stage while kids drew pictures with colored chalk on the pavement by the picnic tables.

Just before noon, Annie, our girls, and assorted friends wandered into the market, shopped, and danced a bit with the little kids before confronting me with the fact that they were all hungry and ready to eat breakfast. Well, by noon, you'd hope so.

We strolled up Main Street, watched some amazing mime performers on the street in front of the Waterbrook tasting room and made our way to Coffee Connection where Greg seated us at one of the big communal tables in the back. The place was packed with Whitman students and their families eating various combinations of breakfast and lunch with the waitresses running from table to table and shouting their orders to the kitchen. Students roamed the tables saying hello to their fellow graduates and meeting their extended families. I mostly just sat and watched the show, marveling at the talent I have for forgetting names and faces.

After lunch we all went off in different directions. Jolie and I went to get her cap and gown—a process that may have taken a full two minutes—and then went off to the college to hear student *a capella* groups sing. We both love live music. The weekend had thus far been a blur of activity, so it was nice to have a couple of hours with the graduating Jolie all to myself.

Annie and the rest of the crowd went to Floyd and Mary's house to pick up the potato salad and chocolate cake Mary had made for us. I like chocolate cake but I love potato salad and Mary makes some of the best potato salad I've ever eaten. After touring Mary's gardens (which are spectacular), Annie and the kids drove straight to the local tire store, got inner tubes and went back out to the farm. They spent the entire afternoon tubing down the river and swimming in some of the deeper pools just upriver from the farm-house.

You were asking about Lindsey, Hannah, Erin, and Elizabeth. Yes, we spent most of the weekend with them and, for the first time, really got to know their families. Lindsey's family hosted dinner on Saturday night for our clan and the seven of them—a welcome break from the graduation crowds and a fitting con-clusion to four years of college-inspired friendship.

I hope we'll be able to keep up with all of Jolie's friends. They made the early days of our move to Walla Walla very comfortable. I don't know how many times I walked into the farmhouse after a trip to the post office to find a fire smoldering in the fireplace and several of these girls huddled up in big comfort-able chairs, wrapped in blankets, pretending to study, but somehow doing it with their eyes closed. We'll miss them.

Sunday morning was cold and rainy—a state of affairs not anticipated by anybody but Hannah's dad who seems to be prepared for anything most all the time. We headed into town for the graduation cere-mony, which was planned as an outdoor event but could be moved inside in the event of inclement weather. Well, thank goodness for that. We'd spent so much time with Jolie's friends and their families that I (and I'll venture a guess, everybody else) had run out of things to say. So, we spent Sunday morning specu-lating about the meaning of "inclement weather," who was going to make the decision whether the ceremo-nies were going inside, and when we'd find out.

I ran to the local drugstore and bought several umbrellas, which I had the pleasure of hauling around with me for the next three hours before the ceremony was to begin. I should have known that it'd clear up as soon as I bought them, and sure enough, the sky started to brighten as I walked out of the store, but not enough that you'd have been comfortable leaving those umbrellas in the car as you went off to get seats in the bleachers set out on the street in front of the Whitman College clock tower.

Annie and the rest of our troop had run off to the Coffee Perk to stay out of the weather with Hannah and her mom while "the dads" went to save seats for the ceremony that didn't start for another hour. When I arrived at the bleachers, sure enough, there was Hannah's dad standing on the top row of seats motioning me to come up. He had umbrellas, towels to wipe off the seats, extra jackets and continuous cell phone contact with Hannah's mom, in case he thought of any other necessities that they could bring when they showed up. I'd left my cell phone in the car and, other than my three brand new umbrellas, was completely unprepared.

After hearing Ron expound on the benefits of sitting in the top row—good view, seat backs (sort of), out from under the trees that would be dripping water on everybody through the entire ceremony even if the rain stopped, etc.—we settled in for a long wait and wondered aloud whether we were wasting our time. It seemed more and more likely that the whole thing was going to move inside and that we'd have to give up the exceptional bench seating we'd worked so hard to claim.

Well, I think the combination of having bought three umbrellas and essentially giving up all hope of an outdoor graduation was too much for the weatherman. Within minutes the drizzle subsided, the cold wind stopped blowing and the sun came out. Miserable turned to glorious. As if on cue, our families showed up trailing balloons behind them and took up their seats along the top row.

Walla Walla loves a party. Any excuse for a gathering is good enough. So it wasn't just a day for Whitman College faculty, students, and their families. It was a day for Walla Wallans to get out in the sun, hear some good music, listen to a couple of mercifully short and surprisingly good speeches, greet their neighbors and then chow down on the huge picnic meal served on the lawns of the school after the students received their papers. I wish you could have been here; you would have loved it.

While we offered our congratulations to the graduates and said our goodbyes to their families, you could see Annie begin to relax. She'd been "on" for the last week working tirelessly on the party and plans for the big event and spent the weekend making sure that everybody around her was having a good time. She started nodding off on our drive back out to the farm.

As we pulled up to the house, she mumbled something about a nap, changed into her blue jeans, a sweater and flip-flops, and headed straight out to the hammock on the porch with a pillow off our bed.

Nobody heard another word from her until well after dinner and the only words she uttered then were "good night, hope everybody had a good time, I'm going to bed" as she rolled herself out of the hammock and stumbled toward our bedroom.

The girls, their friends and I ate chicken sandwiches and Mary's potato salad for dinner out on the porch, had Mary's chocolate cake for dessert which Ben proclaimed to be "awesome," played Frisbee with the dogs, and generally hung out until dark when I said my goodnights and followed Annie's trail of discarded clothing to bed.

It was a memorable weekend and now you know more about it than you wanted to know. I've enclosed a handful of pictures that Annie took; she's written descriptions on the backs of them for you. Maybe you could pass them on to Gary when you've tired of them. Tell everybody in Nashville we say "hi."

Much love,
SAM

It's All About the Meatballs

Dear Dave:

You will get a kick out of this. I stopped by The Oasis this morning for a cup of coffee and sat at the bar with Harold and a friend of his named Buster. Harold is a cattle rancher down the way. I'm guessing he's about 70 but still going strong—tending his herd every day and rounding up calves to take to market. Buster is about the same age and was helping Harold out for a few days while Harold's wife Maureen was in Seattle in the hospital undergoing some medical tests, accompanied by their daughter, Sissy. That way, Harold could stay home and take care of the cattle.

Well, I was just listening along, drinking my coffee and watching reruns of rerides in a professional bull-riding event on the TV above the bar. So, Buster asked Harold if those doctors over in Seattle had found out what was ailing Maureen. Without cracking a smile, Harold says, "Nope, they don't know nuthin' yet but they've figured out it ain't her heart."

"How do they know it ain't her heart?" says Buster.

"Turns out she don't have one," says Harold. "And

they know it ain't her brain, 'cause she don't have one of them neither."

So Buster almost falls off his stool laughing while Deb wags her finger at Harold saying that poking fun at a sick person isn't nice, even if she is your wife. If you run out of entertainment in your life, just go sit at the bar in The Oasis.

Anyway, that's not why I'm writing . . . One of the things I've been struck by is the number of people I've met here in Walla Walla who have decided to give up a life that many would envy to do something they truly love. One of those folks is Gordy who is a winemaker, along with his partner, Myles, at Walla Walla Vintners. These two started making wine as a hobby about 20 years ago. Gordy was an accountant for awhile and then took over his dad's insurance business and did that full time until just a few years ago when he figured out that he liked the insurance business well enough but he loved making wine. So, he up and quit his day job to make wine full time. I've always admired what Joseph Campbell said about "following your bliss" and it seems that Gordy found his and made a gutsy decision to go with it. He says he's never looked back—that it was the best decision he's ever made . . . other than marrying Kate, of course.

Now, I didn't know Gordy during his insurance days, but whatever he was like then, he is now a fellow who's up early to get down to Merchants to have coffee with his buddies before running off to his winemaking duties. He loves his job and it shows in everything he does—from greeting friends and visitors, to making great wines, to teaching his favorite meatball recipe to the uninitiated like me, and then sitting down to a big dinner featuring his handiwork.

Gordy and Myles make great red wines—some of the best in the Valley—and have an almost cult-like following. I was at the winery on Spring Release Weekend hawking my book, and came away amazed at the number of folks I met who have known Gordy and Myles since the early days of their commercial winemaking and come back every year for the new releases.

When you get over here next, you and Susan should take a ride out Mill Creek Road and go see their winery. It's a converted barn with a bunch of outbuildings up on a hill looking out across the Walla Walla Valley as far as a person's eyes can see.

Anyway, that's not why I'm writing . . . Gordy was raised in the Italian community here in Walla Walla— sort of Little Italy on the Prairie. Walla Walla has a very large and active Italian community that grew up here off the foundation of families mostly from two small villages in Italy—Cosenza way down in southern Italy and Linate Pozzolo near Milan in the north.

The way I heard it from Gordy and his Uncle Dave, a gentleman named Luigi Rizzuti immigrated to America in about 1883 from Cosenza to seek his fortune in the California Gold Rush. He arrived in California a little too late to make his fortune there. So, he packed up and headed for the Idaho Gold Rush. He arrived in Idaho a little too late to make his fortune there. So, he settled down in Walla Walla and went to work farming.

By 1900, Luigi tired of his solitary existence and sent

word back to his family that they should come on over to Walla Walla if they wanted something better to do. One of the folks who showed up was Frank Venneri, Luigi's nephew. And then a few years later, Frank sent back for a certain young lady to come over and be his wife, but she was taken, so the family back in Italy had a meeting and sent Josephine Ciarlo instead. (I can only imagine Frank's surprise when Josephine arrived.) Apparently that worked out well enough though, and the family grew thereafter through immigration and local birthing until there was quite a clan of Rizzutis and Venneris all around.

Well, with minor variations, this story was repeated by the Saturno family from just outside Naples and the Tachi family from Linate Pozzolo just outside Milan, and on and on until there was a sizeable community of truck-farming Italians living on small farms way out in the country to the south and west of Walla Walla. To the south, it was pretty much exclusively southern Italians and to the west, northern Italians. The two communities normally maintained their distance from one another; but being good Catholics, they did get together for weekly church services where it's said that the northern Italians sat on the north side of the aisle and the southern Italians sat on the south side. Only at big church events like baptisms, marriages and funerals did this self-inflicted segregation seem to give way to surreptitious mixing encouraged by tables loaded to overflowing with Italian staples, always including meatballs, and casks of homemade wine. And that's what I'm writing you about . . .

Several weeks ago, Annie and I had dinner at Ron and Jamie's house with Ken and Ginger and Gordy and Kate. Now, Ron and Ken and Gordy are all winemakers and winemakers are, by nature, independent sorts who love their wine and their food. Almost any excuse for a big dinner featuring their winemaking and culinary skills will do. Why Annie and I were invited to participate is still a mystery, but we are not inclined to look a gift horse in the mouth—so to speak—so we showed up and had a wonderful time. I won't gush about the food and wine except to say that these winemakers and their better halves put on quite a spread made even more enjoyable by their free-flowing wines.

Well, that's not the reason I'm writing . . . The point is that I was sitting near enough to Gordy at dinner to hear everything he had to say—which was a lot. Over some really tasty roasted chicken, the conversation found its way to Gordy's growing up Italian in Walla Walla. He started out with a few stories about some place called Graybill's, which isn't around any more but was a great place to collect salamanders and make a first rate mud pie. Then we moved on to first grade. We bogged down a bit when we got to third grade, spent some serious time on the fourth grade Valentines party, and wondered a lot about whatever became of his friend Gary from fifth grade. (Some say he became a winemaker too, but I don't really know.) Thankfully, the stories about his sixth grade escapades picked up the pace again.

So, all in all, what Gordy had to say was sort of interesting up to his twenties where we got into a great deal of detail about his education, leaving Walla Walla to live on his own and learning several of life's lessons the hard way, and then starting his accounting career and coming back to Walla Walla.

One thing you learn about Gordy: He is not inclined to leave out many details.

Anyway, as we got up to his later twenties he told us that his mother died much too young and left his father without a helpmate. As Gordy explained it, his dad was pretty much helpless around the house and not inclined to learn house-making skills at his time of life. So, an appropriate number of months after his wife's funeral, Gordy's dad went in search of a new wife and listed the main qualification for consideration as "makes good meatballs." Now we were getting somewhere. Annie and I love good meatballs but have never figured out how to make any worth anointing with a decent tomato sauce.

Several folks have told me that the Italian community pretty much runs on high quality meatballs and nobody makes them better than Marguerite and Betty, both being aunts to Gordy.

Betty, who was Gordy's mother's sister, had been recently widowed. Well, obviously Gordy's dad knew his wife's sister pretty well; she made good meatballs; and she was available. So, Gordy's dad married Betty, and life was good again—meatballs and all.

Gordy says that, at the announcement of any big Italian community event, such as a funeral, Italian folks around here are generally polite enough to ask who died before moving on quickly to "who's making the meatballs?"—which seems to be the more important bit of information. Meatballs are a big deal among the descendants of those early Italian immigrants. Every Italian cook has her favorite recipe and will freely tell you that while "some" other recipes are pretty good, hers has qualities that tend to produce truly superior meatballs.

So, just to participate in a positive way in the conversation, I interjected that Annie and I love meatballs and regularly buy a special brand of frozen ones that we like a lot. Well, for the first time in quite a while now, Gordy was dumbstruck silent while he let that news sink in, and Kate got this little now-you've-done-it grin on her face. In retrospect, I'm not quite sure what I could have said to Gordy that would have been more disturbing.

As he was recovering from the shock, Kate broke the tension by saying that Gordy's meatballs—the recipe having been handed down from Marguerite—were way better than anything you could buy and that Gordy would be happy to have me come over to their house for a meatball-making lesson. "Wouldn't you, Gordy?" she said.

So there I was, enjoying this fabulous meal and mostly scintillating conversation, and managing to get myself invited to Gordy and Kate's house for Gordy's meatball demonstration class. "Not too shabby, McLeod . . . You clever guy," I said to myself.

As I said, Annie and I have made a lot of meatballs in our day, but not any worth talking about—always too hard and dry or so soft and mushy that our meatballs in sauce would turn into a plain meat sauce without any evidence that meatballs had once been there. "What day works for you?" I asked Gordy. "I'll get my calendar out of the car."

Annie would have been embarrassed by my aggressiveness if she weren't such a big fan of my learning new recipes to improve her at-home dining experience—and she loves meatballs.

The following Thursday, I showed up at Gordy's at 5:00pm and we went immediately into their kitchen, Gordy saying that making meatballs required a glass of sangiovese and that I should make a note of it. Like the efficient former accountant that he is, Gordy had all of his meatball ingredients organized in cups and bowls on the kitchen counter around a huge central bowl that we'd use to assemble the meatball mixture. He also had made me a copy of Marguerite's recipe—edited with his own instructions and variations handwritten in the margin. It looked well used. We couldn't get started until I had taken my No.2 sharpened pencil and written, "Glass of Walla Walla Vintners Sangiovese" up in the left-hand corner on my recipe copy.

So then we made meatballs—about 50 of them—and Kate joined us in the kitchen just in time to sample the finished product. All I can say is, "Unbelievable." They were the best meatballs I'd ever eaten—picked out of the pan, otherwise unadorned, on the end of a fork.

Now, it took me a while and a little arm twisting to get Gordy to let me send you this recipe and he only let me do it after I'd gone by to see his Uncle Dave and Aunt Marguerite and gotten her permission, too. So here it is, but you can't share it with anybody else.

Gordy's Meatballs (Via Marguerite)

This recipe makes 40 to 50 meatballs.

Ingredients

2 lbs. Extra Lean Ground Beef
1 lb. Ground Pork
1 c. Breadcrumbs (store bought—OK)
1 c. Freshly-grated Parmigiano Reggiano Cheese
½ c. Chopped Fresh Italian Parsley
6 lg. Eggs—slightly beaten
¾ tsp. Freshly-ground Black Pepper
1 tsp. Salt
2 lg. Garlic Cloves—minced or pressed
4 slices Sandwich Bread
½ c. Milk
1 c. Water (room temperature)
Olive oil to coat the bottom of your frying pan

1. Put the bread and milk in the big bowl and mush up really good with your hands until the bread is no longer recognizable as bread.
2. Then put all the other ingredients, except the water and the olive oil, in the bowl and mush together with your hands until all the stuff is well mixed.
3. Now, here comes the tricky part. It turns out that good meatballs are all about consistency. Add the water a little bit at a time until a ping-pong ball sized bit of the mixture can be rolled into a slightly flattened ball (more like a football that's lost some

of its air) and hold its shape. The meatballs should be pretty moist but not falling apart. I normally end up using all the water but occasionally I need a little less than a whole cup. Anyway, roll the meatballs and put on a plate, covering them with a slightly damp cloth to hold their moisture while you're cooking.

4. Heat a nonstick pan over medium heat and add the olive oil to coat the pan.

5. Cook the meatballs until just slightly browned on both sides (1 to 2 minutes per side). You don't want to cook the meatballs through—just until browned and holding together pretty good.

6. At this point, you can put the meatballs on a cookie sheet and freeze them slightly, then put them in plastic freezer bags, and keep them frozen if you want to.

7. Whenever you're ready to eat them, just make your favorite tomato sauce and drop some meatballs in (2 to 3 per serving) and let them simmer in the sauce for an hour or two until you're ready to eat. (I often get 5 or 6 meatballs out of the freezer, make a simple tomato sauce of fresh tomatoes, garlic, olive oil, and salt/pepper to taste, and then simmer the frozen meatballs in the sauce for an hour or so until the meatballs are cooked through.) Toss with pasta and serve.

Well, I hope you enjoy them. And whatever you do, don't give the meatball recipe to anybody else. Gordy will kill me.

I should be in Seattle for a few days sometime in the next two weeks. I'll give you a call; maybe we can grab dinner. Tell Susan I'll buy.

Best,
SAM

Counting Trees

Note to Readers: A few day after writing this letter, the "School Fire" broke out up in the Blue Mountains about 30 miles east of Walla Walla. The fire burned for almost two weeks. Before firefighters could subdue it, the fire claimed over 41,000 acres of forest land and wheat fields and took down over a hundred farmhouses, cabins and related buildings. From our porch, we could see the huge plumes of smoke blowing over toward Idaho. Mike, who is the subject of this letter, was one of over 1700 people involved in fighting the fire. It's tough work. We thank them.

Dear Byrd:

We really enjoyed your visit. As always, it was good to get to spend some time with you guys. You and Mary were asking about the shrubs and trees that we are planning to plant out on The Land over the next few years. At the time we didn't have a very good answer for you, but now I think a plan is slowly taking shape.

Several weeks ago, Mike (the plant expert fellow I told you about) and his wife, Merry Lynn (who knows as much as Mike, maybe more), came back out to the farm and sat on the porch with Annie and me for a couple of hours to talk about the shrubs and trees we might plant this coming fall. Mike is a biologist by training and works for the U.S. Forest Service on environmental assessment projects up in the Umatilla National Forest. This is the forest that contains the Blue Mountains you saw from your cabin porch. Mike and Merry Lynn have become good friends and have been wonderful about sharing their knowledge (infinitely greater than ours) on local plants and animals.

Anyway, after we'd talked about how the new grasses are doing out in the meadow—surprisingly well given current drought conditions—Mike started talking about what we might do next to improve the wildlife habitat. There are a couple of fairly wet areas between our house and the river. There's a seasonal spring down there that'll support native Coyote Willows, Peach Leaf Willows, Black Hawthorne, Great Basin Wild Rye, Snowberry and Blue Elderberry.

The rest of the property is very dry and, without irrigation water, probably won't support much more than local bunchgrasses, drought-resistant fescues, Tall Wheatgrass and several varieties of sagebrush. Mike did think we might be able to establish a few small groves of ash and Austrian pine out there if we could get some water on them for the first couple of years after we plant them. I'm going to have to check to see if we can get permission to use our modest water rights for that kind of project, so only time will tell. Trees will provide good cover for ground-dwelling critters and perches for birds—particularly the hawks we're relying on to help control the voles and ground squirrels that seem to be thriving out here.

Well, as it happens, the conversation wandered and we got into a bit of Mike's history and how he got interested in biology. Back in 1964, when Mike was just 7 years old, his parents signed up to be missionaries for the Seventh Day Adventist Church. Without any real understanding of what they were getting into (Mike says they were "blissfully ignorant"), the family—Mom, Dad, Mike and younger brother, Joe—boarded a freighter in New York with nineteen other families, bound for the southern tip of Africa. Crossing the Atlantic took twenty-one days. On board the freighter, there was an ornithologist who'd sit with Mike every day on the stern of the ship and help him identify the sea birds they saw along the way.

Mike had always been interested in bugs and birds—probably the result of early childhood education provided by his mom. She'd stick plant and animal flash cards in the crack in the kitchen table at home so they'd stand up and then quiz Mike about them during breakfast.

They arrived in Africa and made the very long train trek to Blantyre, Malawi where they expected to end their travels, only to find that they had another 85 miles to travel—deep into the African bush to a tiny little village called "Carry On" on the banks of the Nkulamadze (N-koola-maud-zee) which means Cold Water River. On arrival, they learned that the area suffered from major problems with malaria and that three previous missionaries had ended their tours of duty there in malaria-induced death.

Without an effective preventative, Mike and his

brother contracted malaria and spent the next two years in the disease's grip—seven days of good health followed by three days of intense headaches, fever, muscle cramps and chills, then another seven days of relative good health followed by another three days of pure hell—week in and week out. As Mike says, it was miserable but most of the villagers were similarly afflicted so nobody really knew that life could have been better.

The boys soon found friends among the village kids and learned the local language full of clicks and guttural trills. They played in the bush where Mike started collecting butterflies that he kept in the African mahogany cases his dad made for him. Before he left Africa, Mike would collect 23 cases of butterflies that would ultimately find their way into collections at Washington State University and The University of Puget Sound.

The village diet lacked protein, so the village kids were encouraged to collect small birds, mice and rats as protein supplements. Apparently the village boys were pretty good with their slingshots and regularly felled birds of all kinds that Mike would get to see before they were handed off to the women of the village for the communal stew pot. With his well-worn copy of *The Birds of Southern Africa* in hand and a pair of clunky Sears binoculars around his neck, Mike wandered the bush identifying the birds they hunted and calling the names out to his younger brother and his friends—leading birding trips at the age of seven.

Over the next couple of years, Mike played deadly

games with Black Mambas, fished in crocodile infested waters, swam with hippos that threatened him with their wide-mouthed yawns, and eluded the guerilla fighters that roamed the bush. You'd love his amazing stories, but they're not really the reason I'm telling you about Mike's history, so I'll leave them for another day. The point is that, in spite of all the difficulties, Mike took every opportunity to exercise his curiosity about the animals around him.

Well, Mike ended up in Walla Walla where he studied biology in college, continued his birding adventures, and through his love of birding, found Merry Lynn, his wife, who loves birding as much as Mike does. He joined the local Audubon Society back in 1979 where he met Merry Lynn, and they are still leading birding trips most every weekend. Their combined birding experience is the stuff of legend around here.

While we were sitting on the porch that day, Merry Lynn identified a Western Kingbird that had just arrived out at the farm after a long flight from South America—a bird that Annie and I had been seeing but not identifying, even with the help of our three thick bird books.

Before he left that day, Mike described the Forest Service projects he's worked on up in the Blue Mountains. It seems that he's walked almost every square hectare of those mountains and knows the plant and animal life up there from the ground up into the tree canopy.

Well, now to the real point of this letter: I spent two

days last week with Mike up in the mountains counting trees . . . yep, that's right, counting trees. Now
before you start with the smart remarks, I'll tell you
that plots have been identified up and down the Blue
Mountain range where there are marked stands of
trees—mostly evergreens—huddled up in the drainage
draws between plateaus. Mike and his Forest Service
buddies regularly hike into these tree stands to examine them and track their health.

On Wednesday, I met Mike at the Ranger Station
here in Walla Walla and we struck out for an area well
up Meacham Creek deep in the middle of nowhere
Oregon. We drove for a couple of hours before enter-
ing the very narrow canyon that contains the creek
and rail tracks of the Union Pacific—leaving barely
enough room for a gravel road that runs parallel to the
tracks and the creek. Then we drove another thirty
minutes or so at about five miles per hour up into the
drainage where we found a spot off the road within
spitting distance of the tracks (and I can't spit very far
at all).

We donned backpacks full of water, GPS location
finding equipment, a Forest Service radio that got
amazing reception everywhere we went, a long measuring tape, a book in which to record the tree health
data, a first aid kit designed to deal with the ill effects
of everything from mosquito bites to cougar mauling,
a very large canister of bear spray, and almonds salted
enough to insure effective water retention.

And we started off walking down toward the creek
until Mike remembered that he'd left his snake stick in

the truck and hustled back to get it while I stood wondering what I was about to step on. When he got back, I inquired as to the need for the snake stick and he explained that we were going to be hiking up a small draw following a small creek that feeds into Meacham Creek. And that's when he told me that Western Rattlesnakes just love to congregate along these creeks.

Okay then, sorry I asked.

At that, we were off again. For the next hour or so we bushwhacked our way up this creek to a point where we heard birds (which Mike identified as Gray Jays) squawking their heads off.

"So, what are they so upset about?" I asked.

"Oh, they're mobbing some predator," Mike said as he pushed toward the ruckus.

"What kind of predator?" I asked.

"Don't know," Mike responded. "Could be anything from an owl, or a hawk, or a snake, or a wolverine to a bear or a cougar. I can't see yet what it is."

"Why do we want to see what it is?" I asked. "If it's maybe something that'll maul us and then eat us, why do we feel the need to deliver ourselves up to it—on a silver platter so to speak?"

"Oh, it's probably not anything that'll bother us," he whispered. "We're getting close now, so keep your wits about you."

"Mike," I said, "I've just forgotten exactly what I should do if it's a big mother bear with cubs that haven't eaten well in a few days. I can't remember whether I'm supposed to run, or stay cool, or roll up on the ground into a fetal ball, or what. What do you think?"

"We're so deep in the brush right here that you don't need to worry about that," he whispered even more softly. "We'd never be able to escape an angry bear in this stuff."

Okay, sorry I asked.

At that point, whatever it was moved off in the brush ahead of us without a sound. "There it goes," Mike said standing up. "Shame we didn't get to see it, whatever it was."

"Yep, a real shame," I said.

And that's when we started up—near as I could tell, straight up. I figured the slope at about 89.5°. Mike said he figured it at maybe 35°.

Now, I haven't told you yet that Mike is a very big guy. But he's mostly muscle and used to traipsing around in the woods. I'm not either of those things. He moved up that slope like an army tank—undeterred by the brush, the soft ground or the loose rock that tripped me up every third step. I struggled up behind him—grabbing tree branches ahead of me to pull my way up that incline. We passed hundreds of trees on our way and that's when I said, in a barely audible voice broken by heavy intakes of oxygen, "What's wrong with these trees—the ones down here at the bottom of the slope? Don't they need their health check up? Why do you guys pick trees at the remotest reaches of human endurance to study?"

It was quiet for a while. Then he said, "Good question." And we moved on.

After an almost interminable climb, Mike stopped,

looked around and announced that we'd arrived. I knelt or collapsed (depending upon your point of view) on the ground. I would have kissed the dirt if I'd been able to catch my breath long enough to pucker my lips.

Mike sat down on the back of a downed tree, pulled out his GPS thing-a-ma-jig and waited for the satellites to line up and tell us where we'd gotten to. It will not surprise you to hear that the canyon walls—the ones we'd just scaled—were so steep that we had very little sky above us. In fact, the slopes were so steep that we couldn't get a GPS reading. That's when Mike said, "Okay, maybe that slope was a little steeper than I thought." (Brilliant deduction, Mike—just brilliant.)

Mike then got out his satellite maps, figured out our location as best he could, recorded the coordinates, retrieved his government-issue measuring tape from his pack, and said, "Let's get on with it."

That, in retrospect, was the beginning of one of the most interesting lectures I've ever attended. As we measured each tree's DBH (diameter at breast height), those trees talked to Mike. Tree type told Mike about the soil type, soil depth and moisture content. The bark told him about the insects and fungi that were constantly attacking it, the woodpeckers that were feeding on the insects, and the damage caused by a small fire in the area several years ago. Their canopies told Mike about the birds and squirrels that lived in the area. Animal droppings told Mike about visitors to the area and how recently they'd visited.

While he listened to the trees and translated for me,

he also heard the calls of resident birds—identifying each from its call and asking me to make a note in the data book. We heard Western Wood-Pewees, Brown Creepers, Chipping Sparrows, Northern Flickers and many other birds' songs. As we wandered through the underbrush on the plot, Mike identified the plants that covered the forest floor—native roses, Black Hawthorne, Indian Paintbrush, Fireweed, Ceanothis (and the California Tortoise Shell Butterfly that feeds on its tannic acid-filled leaves), Big Huckleberry bushes, Nine Bark bushes, and on and on. There was no way to retain it all.

You could tell that Mike was in his element and happy to be there. After I'd caught my breath and managed to swallow my heart back down into my chest, I was happy to be there, too.

It was peaceful there. Aside from the birdcalls, all you could hear was the soft voice of the hot breeze that blew in from the ridge top. And that's what kept us moving. It can get blistering hot up there in the late afternoon. That's why we'd gotten an early start; we needed to get our hiking over with before Sam got heatstroke.

So after a couple of hours, we left that spot—reluctantly. All I could think about was how beautiful a place it was and how I'd probably never see it again. It made you want to linger there and soak up the experience.

Going down was easier on my lungs but tougher on my thigh muscles—the ones that occasionally help me down a flight of stairs. It was slow going until you lost your footing and slid twenty feet on your backside. On the way down, I quizzed Mike about the mammal visitors to the plot—the ones who'd left their droppings for us to examine. Mike figured that there was one big cougar, a small black bear, a herd of elk, numerous mule deer, and a surprisingly large population of chipmunks that probably attracted the owls and hawks Mike had identified from their droppings as well.

And then I asked him why we hadn't seen or heard one of those Western Rattlesnakes that were so prolific in the canyon and he said, "We haven't gotten back to the truck yet; watch where you're walking." After that I did not step in a spot that he'd not stepped in before me. I watched his feet like one of those Northern Harrier Hawks we'd seen (from way up on the ridge) scouting the ground on the canyon floor. Thankfully he did not tell me what is apparently true: The rattlesnakes around here can be so lethargic at times that they miss the first hiker to disturb them and nail the second guy.

Okay, glad I didn't ask.

It was mid-afternoon when we got back to the truck—what the Forest Service folks call a "green rig." We'd been knocking around in the woods for almost seven hours. My peanut butter sandwich tasted pretty good. So did the cold mountain spring water we filled our water bottles with on the way up the canyon. And I've never enjoyed almonds as much as I did that afternoon.

On the drive back to Walla Walla, we listened to the Forest Service radio and all the talk about fires that had begun to spring up in the hot, dry summer air—mostly from violent beginnings as lightening strikes. I'll have to say I was very impressed at how many Forest Service folks are in those mountains every day taking care of the forest—studying tree health, bird migration and habitat, fish numbers, and myriad other things, and watching out for the smoldering tree stump that may just create the next major fire.

And I know now how incredibly hard they work. Mike is in those woods from April until October when the snows pretty much close the place down until the following April. Goodness knows how far he walks in the woods in a season. He does know that he drives about 8,000 miles through the woods each season.

We got back to Walla Walla about 6:00pm and pulled into the ranger station parking lot. I pulled myself out of the rig and touched down on the hot pavement before I realized that one leg was dead asleep and not responding to messages from my brain. It had had enough. I hung on the doorframe for a while before hobbling to my rig for the short drive home.

By 6:30pm I had showered, eaten some dinner from the pots still simmering on the stove, and said goodnight to Annie and Jolie. By 6:35pm, I was in bed snoozing away. I stayed that way until 5:00am the next morning when I got up and headed off to meet Mike for another day in the woods. It was the best night's sleep I'd had in months.

Best,
SAM

All Organic, Free Range, No MSG, Etc.

Dear Wiese:

You are going to be proud of us. After all those years of your preaching on the subject of the myriad ways we are all slowly embalming ourselves with preservatives and missing the flavors of fresh-harvested foods, Annie and I are finally settling into a healthier way of eating. While Annie worries about the additives, I worry about maximizing flavor; so we have struck a balance that's comfortable, but still have a lot to learn.

It has taken us a while to wean ourselves off of the chain grocery stores and find sources of local produce where we've gotten to know the folks and how they raise their animals or grow their fruits, herbs and vegetables. But we are getting there.

Shortly after we arrived here in Walla Walla, we got to know Joan and Pierre-Louis who make goat and sheep milk cheeses up near Dayton (about a 45-minute drive from the farm). We started buying fresh cheeses from them and then found out that they also sell fresh chicken and duck eggs, so we started buying our eggs there as well. (If you've never had a duck egg omelet, remind me next time you're here and we'll cook one up. The duck eggs are pretty rich by themselves, so I mix them about half and half with chicken eggs.)

Well, Joan introduced us to some pigs on a farm up above Dayton. The pigs' diet consists mostly of whey from Joan and Pierre-Louis' fromagerie, and whatever they forage up in the mountains—mostly nuts and roots probably. Joan swore by the quality of those pigs, so we ordered one of them and had it butchered and packaged for our freezer. Now, I don't know for sure; maybe I'm just making this up; but Annie and I both think this pork tastes way better than any store-bought pork.

So, we were telling some of Jolie's friends about that pig and Andrea told us that we should get to know Thundering Hooves, a farm out near us. Turns out they're just a couple of miles south of us on Stateline Road where they raise cows, turkeys, chickens, sheep and pigs—all free-range on certified organic pastures. Now we get most of our meats from them, and again, we think it's much better than what we can buy out of the freezer case at the store.

Then we started going to the Farmers' Market in Walla Walla on Saturdays and got to know Sarah and Adam who have their own organic gardens and supply fresh fruits, vegetables and herbs to members of their Ideal Organics cooperative. We now go into town every Monday afternoon and pick up our box of whatever's in season from Sarah. I'm sure you're tired of hearing this by now, but fresh-picked lettuce is way better than anything we can buy at the store.

Early this morning I took our little male goat—appropriately named "Snacks"—to the butcher. It was a sad occasion; we'd all gotten attached to the little fellow. But, hey, we're farmers now and Snacks was beginning to harass the animals with his constant head butting. Anyway, there'll be free-range goat in the freezer next week. I may be the only one eating it, but I'm looking forward to trying our first farm-raised meat.

So, after talking about this with friends around town, Pat tells Annie and me that we have unwittingly become part of the sustainable farming movement and are pretty good examples now of how more and more consumers are dealing directly with producers where they can get to know more about the foods they're eating and are finding that fresh-bought food is just plain better tasting. So, when we go to the stores these days, it's mostly to buy dish soap, trash bags and toilet paper—where the all-natural alternatives are just a little too natural.

Larry thinks we are on the slippery slope and will soon be wearing hemp shirts and clogs and lashing ourselves to trees up in the mountains to stop the loggers. I kind of doubt that, but hey, stranger things have happened. I haven't protested about much since the '60s, so maybe there's a little fire left in this rusty old boiler. I guess we'll see.

Anyway, come on out to the farm. We'll have a glass of local free-range wine and eat a 100% certified all organic, pasture-finished, no trans fats, no salt added, additive free, antibiotic free meal. In spite of all that, I know you'll like it.

Best,
SAM

Mean People

Dear Fran:

I got a kick out of your last letter. You are right; there really are a bunch of unusual folks wandering around out there on our planet. I run into folks all the time who are clearly seeing things from a very different point of view. My latest encounter with one of them went something like this:

I walked into the grocery store here in Walla Walla where "annoyance" normally equates to having to wait while one person checks out ahead of you. That's about as bad as it gets. As I was just writing to somebody the other day, we don't go to the store much anymore for food, but there are still some things that we can't buy from our farming and ranching neighbors, and have to get at the store in town.

I got a cart. I started for the aluminum foil aisle. I got halfway down the aisle when I came upon a rather large man whose overloaded cart filled up one half of the aisle and whose rear end filled up the other half. He seemed to be studying up on plastic garbage bags. Being a reasonable sort, I figured he'd look up in a minute, see me, and move his cart or backside so I could pass. Well, it wasn't happening. I knew he could feel my presence by the way he tilted his head as I approached, but he was not making eye contact and I was beginning to feel some annoyance at the stubbornness I was facing.

Now, in my former big city life I'd have said something to the guy like, "You might be surprised to hear this, but there are other people in the world." This kind of accurate but sarcastic statement would get a rude reply. Then I'd huff about a bit, and he'd huff about a bit, and gradually we'd work a situation involving mild stalemate into something worse and end up passing each other while glaring at one another, only to find that we'd run into each other again in the next aisle.

But that is not my way any more. After those little battles in the past, I'd go from bewildered to angry to feeling a little bad about my own behavior, to giving myself a lecture on patience and conflict resolution. I'd decide that the next time I ran into this kind of annoying behavior, I'd stop, count to ten and then handle the situation with grace—trying to see things from the other person's point of view. I was trying to teach myself that there's more to life than getting where you want to go on time; that patience is a virtue; that all we need is love.

So, here I was, feeling aggravated in the grocery store in good-natured little Walla Walla, and for the first time in my life, I caught myself before I reacted with sarcasm. I stood patiently—not even tapping my foot or drum-rolling my fingers along the cart handle. I felt a bit proud of myself. I tried to think why it was that he was not letting me pass. Maybe getting the right garbage bags was the solution to some emergency? (But he didn't look the least bit anxious.) Or maybe getting the right garbage bags was so taxing his brain that he couldn't think about garbage bags and moving aside at the same time—all circuits busy, so to speak? I was just beginning to buy into this point of view when he looked directly at me—staring a little longer than necessary—and rolled his eyes before going back to studying garbage bags without giving up an inch of aisle space.

At that, I recognized the taste of venom rising in my throat, but again, I caught myself; I took several deep breaths; I conjured up a vision of lying on a white sand beach in the Caribbean with a cold beer in the little cooler next to me; and refused to rise to the bait.

Now, to be honest, I knew that I'd switched over from a genuine interest in his point of view to a little holier-than-thou kind of refusal to let this jerk get the better of me, but I still had not responded with sarcasm and that was progress.

So, I said, "Can I help you with something? You seem terribly confused and lacking in decision-making skills." So, okay, I did let loose with just a little bit of sarcasm, but I smiled as I said it and tried to look genuinely helpful.

At this, the guy gave me a withering stare and reached across to his basket where he grabbed hold of the side of it and went back to studying garbage bags. The message was pretty clear—I'd be allowed to pass when he was good and ready for me to or when hell froze over, whichever came later.

Well, that's when mild irritation started flowing into vigorous annoyance. (Annie says I was just plain mad and that the big words are getting in the way of conveying my meaning. But I'm trying to improve my vocabulary so I'm testing out big words from time to time.) So, back to the story . . . I could feel my ears turning red and the hair standing up on the back of my neck. I could feel adrenaline-induced strength surge into the hands that I'd use to strangle this slug.

Thank goodness I didn't have to kill him. About that time the proverbial little old gray-haired lady turned the corner into our aisle and started toward us. She saw the jerk and his cart. She saw the rage in my contorted facial expressions. Without hesitation she rammed the jerk's cart with hers, pushed by, said loud enough for the entire store to hear, "Get your ass out of my way," and then turned to me and said, "Now you can go on by, Sonny." Which I did . . . while the jerk fumed.

So, I say, what was the lesson in all this? Patience did not seem to be a virtue. Love was not all that was needed. In-your-face-I-won't-put-up-with-your-bullshit seemed to win the day and right the injustice. But something tells me that this lesson is not going to find its way into any of the "how to" books on living the virtuous life. It's something to think about.

Well, I thought you'd enjoy that—an instance of finding a mean person right here in Walla Walla. So, okay, we do have . . . one . . .

Best,
SAM

Power's Out

Dear Carl:

After listening to your rant about getting things done in the big city, I thought you might get a kick out of the phone conversation I had yesterday. Like you, I'm a guy conditioned by experience to expect the least from the electric company's customer service folks.

Well, yesterday the power went out here at the farm. I didn't know whether it was just us or a more general blackout. In the city you just yell out the window to your neighbor to find out whether they lost power too, but out here in the hinterlands you can't yell loud enough for the neighbors to hear. And it was daytime, so you couldn't just look out across the pasture to see if the neighbors' lights were on. So, I figured I'd call the electric company hotline.

While I was looking for the phone number in the Walla Walla phone book, I started thinking that this was going to be a painful exercise. I figured I'd call and get a machine that'd tell me to hold onto my shorts and just wait for the next available customer service representative and that the estimated wait time would be longer than I could imagine. Then, after my ear started hurting from pressing the phone into it for so long and after my arm went numb from holding the receiver all the time I was waiting, somebody would come on the line and ask me for my social security number—as if they somehow really needed it.

Then, of course, you find out that the social security number question is just the beginning of a twenty questions game you don't want to play—where were you born, what's your grandma's maiden name, which of your pets is your favorite, what's your mistress' full name and phone number, does your wife know, how much is it worth to you to keep the information you're providing confidential, and on and on . . .

And after you get through all that, the guy tells you that your last electric bill is past due and you tell him that you're on "auto pay" so they control when they get paid. Then the guy asks you to hold while he checks into it and before you can plead with him not to put you on hold, he does. And you sit again, and start to tap your foot.

After another interminable wait during which you listen to hard rock that sounds like it's coming to you through a bad radio signal, the guy comes back on the line and says that your credit card company is not accepting the "auto pay" bill—which just means that "auto pay" really isn't—and you have to go online and reset your "auto pay" after you get things straightened out with your credit card company; and then you can call back and wait too long again for a real person to talk to, and then you can play twenty questions again, and then ask the guy about the power outage only to find that "they're working on it and don't know when the power will be back on."

So, I found the electric company's number up in Dayton—not a hotline, just the regular phone number. And I dialed. It rang once or twice and a guy answered saying, "This is Ron; can I help you?"

So I tell Ron, our power is out. He asks where we live and I tell him Detour Farm and he says oh yeah, that place you just built out near Lowden and I say yes, that's the place. Then he says he's the guy who ran power across the neighbors' field to our building site and we have a nice chat about how we like the new place and how he's welcome to come out and see how it all turned out. So, after the pleasantries, which are essential to the beginning of any conversation in this part of the world, he says that there's been a car wreck out on the highway that took out an electric pole and they expect to have the power back on within the hour.

And I say okay—really appreciate your help. Then he says that there may be other folks calling with the same question, so he better get his phone back on the hook, so folks won't get a busy signal. And I thank him again and say goodbye.

The whole process took maybe two minutes; we had a nice chat; and everybody went away happy.

So, are you still wondering why we like Walla Walla so much? Tell Jan and the kids we say "hi."

Best,
SAM

Back to Nature

Dear Jeff:

Annie and I enjoyed your letter about camping in the back yard with your grandchildren. You and Rhonda are good sports. Next time, you can borrow our air mattresses—the ones we slept on for a few nights when we first moved over here to Walla Walla. In fact you can have them; if I never have to sleep on one again, it'll be too soon for me.

I took one of the mattresses camping a few weeks ago after Marshall twisted my arm and convinced me that a little father/daughter bonding time would be good for us. I found that, after sleeping on the ground—"riding out the night on a cloud" according to the mattress package—I could get my body back to normal by noon if I took an overdose of ibuprofen as soon as I rolled off the mattress and moaned my way to a standing position.

Now, before I go on, you should know that Marshall has never been a big camper. I think she and one of her little girlfriends slept out in the back yard once when Marshall was about 10 years old. If I remember correctly, they lasted about half an hour out there by themselves. Nonetheless, about two months ago, Marshall and several of her friends went camping for a weekend and she loved it. She has been trying to convince somebody to go with her again ever since. That's when she hooked me with the "we haven't done anything special—just the two of us—like you're always doing with Jolie and Summer" guilt trip. Well, I'm not "always doing" something special with Jolie and Summer, but she was right that we hadn't done a father/daughter outing in a while.

So, I quizzed Marshall about where we'd go and what we'd need and she assured me that she'd borrow the equipment and bring it with her from Ellensburg on Friday night. She'd spend the night with Annie and me out here at the farm and the two of us could leave early Saturday morning. A friend of Marshall's had recommended that we camp near the source of the Tucannon River—a trip that would involve about an hour and a half's drive from the farm and an hour's hike into a meadow where we could pitch our tents.

So, long story short, the fateful Saturday morning arrived. I was already packed, so I hopped out of bed, dressed, and hauled my stuff out to the truck. Well, wonder of wonders, Marshall was out there ahead of me, all ready to go. Mentally, I'd prepared myself for an extra half hour's worth of coaxing Marshall out of bed. But that was not necessary. She was up, excited and ready to get on with it. We said our goodbyes to Annie and the dogs, jumped in the truck and took off.

Being a half hour ahead of the game gave me the bright idea of stopping in Dayton at The Panhandler for a little breakfast to stoke us for our expedition. Marshall loves eggs and bacon about as much as I do, so she was up for it as long as I promised I wouldn't strike up a conversation with the folks sitting at the next table and take up the morning gabbing. So, I made my promises and we pulled in.

The place was packed with Saturday morning diners so we grabbed two seats at the counter and bellied up for the big breakfast. Greta took our orders after pouring us each a big mug of coffee. I had the chicken fried steak with biscuits and gravy (which comes on a full plate foundation of hash browns just so you don't go away hungry) while Marshall went for the cheese omelet and hash browns—her all time favorite breakfast combo.

The fellow sitting next to Marshall was a young guy named Luke and he was making small talk with her while I paged through the newspaper that'd been left on my stool by the previous occupant. And that led the two of them into a conversation about the father/daughter trip we were on—which was a roundabout way of explaining to Luke why Marshall would not be staying in Dayton that night and why she would not be available to "hang out." And that got them off on talking about where we were planning to camp and I noticed that Luke seemed very impressed.

Now, I am always promising myself that I'll start listening to the little twinges of discomfort I get about upcoming difficult situations before I get into them. When I look back on my life and the few truly harrowing experiences I've had, they were all preceded by little hints that I should not go there—wherever "there" was at the time. I've read enough books to know that I'm not the only one who gets these little premonitional warnings; it just seems that other folks are a lot better at listening to them than I am.

I'd been a little skeptical when Marshall's friend said that it was only an hour and a half drive into the trailhead and then an easy hike into the meadow—about another hour she'd said. And now I'd noticed a look on Luke's face that made me wonder why he was so impressed with our mission. But, as usual, I was letting these little warnings pass me by.

So, Marshall said goodbye to Luke and then whispered to me that he was "kinda cute" while I was paying Greta for our breakfast and getting directions from her on which road to take out of Pomeroy on our mission into the back country. And we drove on toward Pomeroy where we hit the hour and a half driving time milestone. It was only 10:30am so, what the hay, if it took us a little longer to get to the trailhead, so what? After filling the rig with diesel fuel (which is supposed to be cheaper than gasoline but never is) and stopping for a more detailed map at the Pomeroy Ranger Station, we pressed on, up Peola Road, which turns into Mountain Road which takes you up, up, up on switchbacks to the top of the world along Scoggin Ridge.

Both Marshall and I were awestruck at the views out across the Palouse Hills to the north and the vast expanse of evergreens to our south. It was cool up there, maybe 60°, and a constant breeze blew in from the southwest. We stood on a rock outcropping at a turnout and let the undersides of big white fluffy clouds pass overhead shading us momentarily from the bright sun. I would gladly have pitched out tents right there—and we should have . . .

On we drove, now at the two-plus hour mark, but who's counting? It was slow going on gravel roads that were well maintained but forever winding along the ridge tops. It was a bit like riding a roller coaster in slow motion. And then we arrived at Teal Springs Campground, which boasted commanding views out toward Dayton. I would gladly have pitched our tents right there—and we should have . . .

We pressed on . . . and, well, here's Annie again, looking over my shoulder as I write, wondering what I'm boring you with and telling me that there's enough "pressing on" in this letter already and I should get on to the point. So I'll just skip the rest of the pressing on and tell you that after a total driving time approaching three hours we came to the end of the road at Hard To Get To Ridge—yep, it's true; I'm not making that up.

We parked in a small bare dirt turnout, grabbed our backpacks and started off downhill on what looked to be the trail to the meadow but turned out to be a short trail to nowhere. So we went back to the car and re-consulted the map where we found our error, and struck out south along the meadow trail, which, if we'd been paying attention at all, we'd have noticed was marked by a nice little sign.

Now, for some reason, I've always thought of going south as going more downhill than uphill. But unfortunately that thinking was wrong. Marshall walked, and I struggled, up, up, up along a trail that didn't look but so well used. Thank goodness for all of the beauty concentrated in that spot because otherwise it'd have been awfully hard not to devote my entire attention to the fact that my heart was trying to jump out of my chest through my mouth. Marshall was just chatting on about how beautiful it was and how much fun we were having while I managed the occasional nod between gasps for thin air to fill my lungs.

Even though it was very cool up there in the forest with the constant breeze, I was shedding clothing at every water stop and trying to find room for it in the backpack.

I tied a T-shirt around my forehead to keep the steady rivulets of sweat from running directly into my eyes. I was so hot that, even in 60° weather, my sunglasses were permanently fogged. While Marshall noted wildflowers and birds, and all manner of other little creatures, I trudged on gasping for air, trying to see the trail through the mist on my glasses and wondering how long it would take Marshall to hike back to the truck, drive back into cell phone coverage, and summon help while I suffered through my all-but-certain massive heart attack.

After about an hour and a half of the nearest thing to torture I can imagine, we came to the top of the ridge and, once again, between gulps of thin air, I was bowled over by the incredible views. A small ground squirrel ran up on a rock beside us and gnawed on a large seedpod of some sort while Marshall and I took it all in. A golden eagle soared over our heads, riding the updrafts almost to the point of disappearing. I will never forget that day. Sitting there next to my daughter, on top of the world, in silence broken only by the faint whisper of wind and occasional chatter from our ground squirrel friend—well, what can I say, it was a wonderful moment. That trudge to the top of the ridge was worth every painful step.

After our little rest, we hoisted up our backpacks and followed the trail which ran right along that ridge top through pine forest that broke occasionally into small meadows full of tall grasses, lupine and Indian Paintbrush with hundred-mile views as backdrop. It was spectacular. And then the trail started down . . .

You know, I don't really know what we were thinking. Why didn't my brain say, "Hey, wake up. You're going down. And it's steep. And you're going to have to come back up this tomorrow. And it's not going to be pleasant . . . In fact, it's going to be awful . . . Wake up. Why not just camp back up on that ridge top? It's pretty up there . . . It won't be any prettier wherever we're headed . . ."

Down, down, down, we went. It was so easy. So effortless. You could enjoy the cool of the shade, see the wildflowers, follow the little stream that was the beginning of the Tucannon River, look for the small rainbow trout hiding behind the rocks that littered the stream bottom, and soak up that feeling of great calm that comes from walking in the wilderness.

After another hour or so, we came into the meadow that was to be our home for the night. It was long and narrow, protected by high ridges on either side, with a honeysuckle-lined creek running down its middle. I don't know what little yellow flower was blooming, but there were wildflowers everywhere and tiny orange butterflies by the thousands. You could almost hear Julie Andrews singing in the wind.

It took Marshall about ten seconds to get her hiking boots off, find a comfortable grassy spot on the bank to lie on and get her feet in the creek. And I wasn't far behind. I fell down on the bank next to her wondering when the feeling would return to my legs and how many layers of my precious skin had been removed by the backpack straps that I'd not taken the time to adjust properly.

It was mid-afternoon, so our little two-and-a-half hour trip had really taken the better part of six hours and we were exhausted, a little hungry and thirsty. I grabbed my remaining water bottle (I'd consumed one on the way in) and two granola bars from the bottom of my pack and was reminded that I'd managed to wedge a bottle of wine between layers of clothes in the bottom of the pack.

So, we just sat and when all got quiet again, the wildlife came out to greet us. At one point we could see six female elk with four newborns, about thirty mule deer, a rather small moose with stubby antlers, two skunks, a bunch of wild turkeys, and all manner of small birds that we couldn't begin to identify. While I walked the edge of the meadow looking at various types of mushrooms and consulting my new mushroom guide, Marshall curled up on the creek bank and went fast asleep. We had the place to ourselves and life was good, until . . .

The roof caved in on us. A thunderstorm rolled in over that little valley like a freight train and before we knew it the wind was blowing so hard you couldn't walk into it. We gathered up our packs and carelessly strewn stuff and ran into the trees behind us just in time to escape torrential rain and ping-pong ball sized hail that came crashing out of the sky. The rain and fog rolled down the ridge to our south and obliterated our view. Marshall had found her rain jacket and a sweater and had gotten them on before she got soaked but I wasn't so lucky. I got drenched while feeling around in the bottom of that pack for my hooded windbreaker, but I was trying to do so without getting the other stuff wet. By the time I found it, it wasn't really worth putting it on except to keep the wind from blowing straight through me.

And that's when we noticed that our picture-perfect little creek was starting to look like something to be afraid of. Water came in great gushes from above us and the creek turned into a roiling river in seconds. Marshall and I, cold and very wet, retreated further into the trees, going up again, dragging our drenched packs along with us.

The hail storm was so fierce that we felt we were inside a popcorn popper—little balls of ice bouncing all over the place and occasionally plunking one of us on the head. When it was over, our area in the trees was several inches deep in ice and our meadow looked like the summit on Mt. Everest. And the temperature was headed south, way south—fast.

While the dark clouds were clearing overhead and letting a little sunshine in, the sun was low enough now that it was getting dark in that little valley. There we were—cold, wet, and hungry again, with dusk coming on faster and earlier than we'd expected. Marshall suggested we hike back up to the truck and take refuge back home at the farm, and it took me only a nanosecond to nod my head; but there was no way back up; our little path was buried under the ice.

So, we got out our pup tents and started the grim task of clearing two spots on the icy ground under the trees with our bare hands. Marshall's hands turned bluish pink and you could see the pain etched in her face. But she was a real trouper and just plugged away at making us a camp for the night. It wasn't pretty but within a few minutes we had tents up, deflated air mattresses on the tent floors as an extra layer of protection between us and the sopping wet, cold ground, our sleeping bags unrolled, extra layers of clothes on and our shivering bodies inserted into the bags trying desperately to warm up. We could converse through the tent flaps while we studied the insides of our individual cocoons wondering how that thin plastic could possibly protect us from the raw night that was descending on us as the sun sank lower over a western horizon that we could only picture in our minds.

And then the real bombshell landed: "Hey Dad," Marshall says. "What's for dinner?"

I assumed she was joking—she had to be joking—so I just played along. "Oh, we're starting with Oysters Rockefeller, then a nice mixed greens salad with a

French vinaigrette dressing, followed by broiled trout with a lemon butter herb sauce served on a lemon risotto, and finally Key Lime pie for dessert."

"No, really Dad," she chirped. "What are we having?"

And that's when we both sat bolt upright and stared at each other in disbelief.

"You've got to be kidding," I said.

"About what," she said.

"About dinner," I said. "You brought it, right?"

"No, I brought the camping gear including a little single burner stand," she said, a question rising in her mind. "You didn't bring the food?"

"We have a problem," I said. "I have two more stale granola bars in my pack plus a bottle of wine. That's my menu for dinner. What's yours?

At that, Marshall started rifling through her pack, hoping against hope that she'd find something to eat in there. And she did—a half-eaten Payday candy bar from her last camping trip. And that's when she started laughing, gradually getting herself to the point where she couldn't breathe. And that's when I started laughing so hard that I alternated between laughing and hiccup fits.

There we were sitting in our tents in the middle of a melting ice field, still shivering from the cold, laughing at the absurdity of it all—we were going to be dining on granola bars followed by one modest bite of a candy bar and we'd wash it all down with a shared bottle of red wine. Well, at least we weren't going to starve to death.

So that's where we were and that's just the way it was. Marshall got out two little fold-up bowls, two collapsible cups and several sections off her toilet paper roll to use as napkins. I found the two granola bars and opened the bottle of wine. We may not have been prepared for our night in the wilderness but we were prepared to open a bottle of wine. As hungry as we were, those granola bars went pretty well with the wine. While we ate slowly so as to prolong the enjoyment of our gourmet meal, Marshall heated up the remaining half of her candy bar in a small pot on her one-burner stand and made a great production out of serving up small bites for each of us in our fold-up bowls.

We had a great time talking about how stupid we were, what they'd eaten on her last camping trip, what we'd have for breakfast when we returned to civilization in the morning, where she was going in China to study salamanders, how she was liking college, what she was thinking about doing after college, how she was getting along with her boyfriend, how her mom and I liked farm life, whether it got lonely out on the prairie without the girls to make our lives interesting, and on and on . . .

It was a very special night in spite of our predicament and I think we both went to sleep—still shivering—glad that we'd made the trek.

Thankfully the night was uneventful. The sun didn't really reach into our little valley until about 8:00am, so we slept in without knowing it. It didn't take long to get packed and we didn't have to worry about doing the breakfast dishes. We checked the area one last time, washed our faces in that cold little creek and started the climb back to the summit of the ridge.

It was almost lunchtime when we walked back into The Panhandler and took our seats at the bar. We had talked all the way back about the pancakes we were going to have for breakfast, with a side of waffles, and maybe some biscuits, and the chicken fried steak, hash browns, and a few omelets—maybe one of each kind they served—and orange juice and coffee. We were famished. There was Greta, looking at us like she was seeing ghosts. "Weren't you two in here for breakfast yesterday?" she said.

"Yes, we were," said Marshall.

"And weren't you going camping or something up in The Blues?" Greta continued. "Yes, you were," she said answering her own question. "Well, how was your trip?"

"It was great," I said as I slumped onto the counter feeling a little faint. "Can we order some breakfast?"

And Marshall started laughing so hard she couldn't breathe, all over again.

We'll never forget that little outing. They should all be so memorable.

Best,
SAM

A Walla Walla Moment

Dear Dad:

Yes, we had a great time in Montana. The weather was picture perfect—80s during the day and low 60s at night. All of our old ranch friends were back; so we had a big time catching up with them, fishing, hiking and doing way too much eating.

Anyway, we're back home in the swing of things, and I thought you would appreciate what happened to me yesterday. You're probably thinking an old retired guy gets up in the morning without a plan and goes wherever the wind happens to blow him that day. Sometimes you'd be right, but not as often as you think. I've always heard that work expands to fill the time available and I am now living proof that it's true. Somehow my days are chock full of stuff that keeps me busy—mostly stuff that I enjoy doing.

So, yesterday I had a plan. I'd made my list and got up early to get things done. That's when John called and changed the course of my life—at least for a few hours.

What you don't know is that several weeks ago,

John had taken my picture for a display that we're going to put in bookstores to hold, and hopefully help sell, my book. He couldn't call me while we were in Montana, so he was laying for me when we got back. He called to say that the picture he'd taken hadn't turned out very well and that I needed to come into town so he could take another one.

Well okay, it was for a good cause—selling more books—so I told him I'd be in his shop as soon as I could get there. I hopped in the truck and headed down the driveway where I spied Jack on a mammoth-sized combine as big as our house headed down Detour Road. He was just passing the end of our driveway going toward town like I was. So I waved and pulled in behind him. I figured I'd be able to pass once we got around the curve in the road and I'm guessing that's what he thought too.

Now, we don't get much traffic out our way. I'd be surprised if ten cars pass by The Land on a given day; but yesterday, traffic was just streaming down sleepy little Detour Road. Jack couldn't pull off the road to let me by unless he wanted to take that combine for a swim in the irrigation ditch. So Jack poked along and kept waving his hand to keep me from trying to pass because he could see all that oncoming traffic, while all I could see was the ass end of the combine.

I comforted myself with the fact that it's only about a mile from our driveway to the intersection with McDonald Road where I'd surely find room to pass. I reminded myself that it wouldn't likely change the course of human evolution on this planet if I didn't get another picture taken right away—maybe ever. But like I was saying, unimportant things can take on importance when they are, in spite of their unimportance, the most important things on your "to do" list. You'll remember that I said I'd found lots of things to keep me busy over here in Walla Walla—mostly things that I like to do. I never said that they were important things.

So, anyway, we got to the intersection with McDonald Road and that's where we found out what the deal was. Turley (and no, I don't know where he got that name), our friendly county police officer, had pulled his patrol car across that intersection and was directing traffic from Highway 12 down McDonald Road and onto Detour Road headed east. There'd been a big accident out on the highway. A farm truck had rolled across a train trestle where it was somehow stuck between the railroad tracks. A tow truck had had to back across Highway 12 to get enough leverage on the stuck truck to pull it free. And that's when the county police had been called into action to stop traffic on the highway or divert it—which they'd done.

The good news was that Turley didn't think it'd be too long until things got back to normal and he could let Jack pull the combine off onto McDonald Road which would leave the road to town clear for those of us with important business to attend to. So we waited . . . and waited . . . and waited. Turley would periodically listen in on his walkie-talkie and feed us news, which mostly boiled down to "they're still working on it."

Well, I hate to admit that I can be a little slow in the head sometimes, but it finally dawned on me that I could probably turn around, head west back down Detour Road to its other intersection with the highway, head east into town on the highway, get sidetracked south down MacDonald Road and have Turley direct me back onto Detour Road headed east (but on the other side of Jack and his combine) with nothing but open road between me and town.

Well, I shouldn't have taken so long to figure that out because, by the time I started looking around to see if I could make a U-turn, I saw that cars were now backed up from beyond our farm on Detour Road all the way back to where I was stuck. Nobody on Detour Road was going anywhere, no matter which direction they were headed.

So, what the hay, I climbed down out of my rig and started craning my neck with everybody else to see if I could figure out what had messed up the traffic headed west. That's when I overheard Turley saying to Troy and Judy and Gene and Tom and the rest of the crowd now gathered around Turley's patrol car that Jim, who'd not been aware that cars were being detoured onto Detour Road, had seized on that time to move his cattle—all of them—down Detour Road to his Lowden Gardena Road pasture about a half mile down the way.

Now I reckon it was just bad timing but I could see how a paranoid kind of person might muse on the possibility that this was some kind of impromptu farmer-rancher conspiracy to derail commerce in Walla Walla and hold us all hostage until wheat subsidies were improved. Well, thankfully that's not what it was.

It took Jim about half an hour more to get his cattle moved and by then Turley was getting word that he could pull out of the intersection and let traffic take its accustomed course because the truck stuck at the railroad trestle had been set free and the highway had been cleared of impediments to vehicular progress.

So after saying goodbye to Turley and all the neighbors, I hopped back in the rig and trucked into town—arriving at John's shop just 93 minutes later than I'd told him. In true Walla Walla fashion, John just shrugged up his shoulders and said "no problem" and that we needed to find Brian down at the furniture store to see if he was free to take the picture because the two of them had figured out that the picture-taking problem we were having was unrelated to my poor looks and probably the fault of John's camera.

So we ambled off down the block to Brian's store where he greeted us, put his 14-year-old son, Trevor, temporarily in charge, and led us into his makeshift photography studio in a storage room up on the third floor where Brian quickly took pictures of me until both Brian and John were saying "that's probably as good as it gets" about one of the shots they could see in the back of the camera.

At that, Brian led us back to the front of the store and told Trevor to mind the place while he went with us up to John's store to help with my pictures. Now, what I didn't know, but found out on the stroll to John's shop, was that Brian had never hardly taken pictures until about a month and a half ago, but had gotten a fancy camera for his birthday (that he gave himself) and had taken about 8,000 pictures in his first month of being a photographer—no joke. Brian was finding that there weren't enough computers in Walla Walla to store his collection so he was working with a guy down in Athena, Oregon to see if they couldn't string together a bunch of hard drives to get him out of his storage bind.

Back at John's shop—now just about a half day off plan—we all huddled around John's fancy photo enhancing computer to see if we couldn't make me look "a little more interesting" than I normally appear to be.

So, now this is becoming a fascinating experience. There on the screen is me—a full frontal shot. And this computer can make me look like John Wayne if that's what we want to do. The possibilities were endless. John's significant other, Cherilyn, has now joined us along with Candace who's been helping me with the editing of my books. The two of them had been talking about another project that Candace was working on but they heard Brian and John laughing at my picture and found the opportunity to "fix" my looks an irresistible one.

Unflattering comments about all my physical flaws were flying without coordination until Cherilyn held up her hand and announced that we should start at the top of my head and work our way down to my toes where it was clear that, in sandals, I should have clipped my toenails before going in to have my photo shoot. But, she said, we'd get to that little problem later.

Cherilyn's first suggestion was that John somehow resize my head—that it was way too fat (correction: big) and looked out of proportion to the rest of my body. And that's when they all turned to look at me and agreed that I really do have a big head that really is out of proportion to the rest of my body—except, according to Brian, that my head does fit nicely with my stomach. And that led Candace to my defense saying that I really didn't look "all that big-headed" and that we should just leave well enough alone.

Next it was my eyebrows. Had I ever considered having them plucked? Could John work his magic and make them a little less bushy? Maybe I could ask Ellen, my barber, to trim them up a bit?

Then it was my beard and the "fullness of my cheeks." Maybe John could add a little shadow so as to create something like the hint of the cheekbones that are well hidden beneath my "fleshy" cheeks.

And then it was my shirt, which, according to John, looked like it needed a good ironing. And didn't I have another pair of blue jeans—maybe ones that weren't quite so "full figured," according to Candace? Or "baggy," according to Brian? And had I thought about washing my feet before getting my picture taken?

Well, not only was it an experience, but it was as close as I've ever come to an out-of-body experience. It was like taking your body into a body shop for repairs where the wizard at the computer keyboard who's an expert at "photo enhancement" could, and did, with a deftly handled mouse, de-fat my fat head, trim my eyebrows, create high cheekbones out of dimpled fleshiness, extend my neck to make it look like I have one, iron my shirt, flatten the belly, un-bag the baggy blue jeans and clean and clip my toenails. He even removed an ink stain from my left pants leg.

I had to admit that I looked almost presentable. The group applauded John's handiwork and disassembled as quickly as it had assembled. Brian left, saying that his son was probably taking a snooze on one of the new mattress sets that had been delivered earlier that morning. Candace and Cherilyn went back to their project and John said he had to get to the Rotary lunch where he was presenting some sort of award.

So there I was—staring at the new, improved Sam—a guy who looked good, but only vaguely familiar. After taking in the improvements for a little while, I said to myself, "If the new guy can sell books, so be it." And I walked back out onto the street where I headed over to Ze Bagel and got one of their famous ZeMelts piled high with ham and cheese. I was starving.

Best,
SAM

Hal's Head

D ear Anna Neal:

I re-learned a valuable lesson on last week's family vacation to Montana:

Always tell the truth . . . and *never round up*.

As you know, I have a slight tendency to gird the facts in my storytelling. Up to this point in my life, I have not considered modest exaggeration a fault. I have always thought of it as a way of enhancing the quality of life of anybody who'd listen to the important things I have to say.

Now, Annie is different. She has always taken an opposing view on fact enhancement. She considers it unadulterated lying . . . bordering on sin. She is always telling me that my lying is going to land me in a heap of trouble some day. Well, I never believed her—at least not until last week when I saw the consequences of misleading the public, up close and personal.

The McLeod family went on vacation to Montana for the first time about 15 years ago. Annie is looking over my shoulder and she says it was really just 14 years ago. I am saying that I meant 15 to be a general figure covering a few years either way, but Annie is saying that I'm climbing out on that slippery slope of lying awfully soon after re-learning the wages of sin. And that she is surprised at my *rounding up*.

So, okay, without arguing about it, let's just say that about 14 years ago we started going to Montana on vacation to a guest ranch that offered great hiking, trout fishing, horseback riding, modest but comfortable cabins, and good home cooking served family style. There were no square dances, no cowboys singing by the fire, and no hot tubs—which is just the way I like it.

We went year after year after year, the same week each year, with families from every corner of the US of A who were doing the same thing. The consequence of this annual togetherness was that our ranch friends became family to us. We only saw each other that one week out of a year; but after a few years of being thrown together day and night for a whole week each year, arriving at that ranch was like greeting family at a family reunion without fear of impending family squabbles. It was our little slice of heaven on earth and our whole family loved going. After a while, our kids started calling the other kids in the group their "cousins."

Well, unfortunately that very special place fell victim to the passage of time and the laws of inheritance, and was sold last year to a bunch of big shots who closed the place as a guest ranch and turned it into their own private fishing camp. That left our ranch family group high and dry, and forced us to go searching for another ranch that could accommodate all of us—approximately about roughly 25 of us. (I don't think Annie can find fault with that sentence but she is working on it.)

Anyway, long story short, we did find another ranch south of Bozeman, near Big Sky, that turned out to offer much the same program as our other ranch and could accommodate us if we could all come the first week in July. So we all signed up—all approximately about roughly 25 of us—and arrived at our new ranch a week ago last Sunday.

Now, several of our extended ranch family are fishermen (actually "fisherpeople"). I am one of them. So is Annie as long as she can wear her headphones, listen to Motown oldies and catch fish with predictability. Then there are John and John and Susan and Steve and Hal and very occasionally Mary, and Paul and Barbara. So, to get on with it, there are a bunch of us fisherpeople and we represent only the tip of the vacationing fisherpeople iceberg. There are bunches of fisherpeople everywhere in the vicinity of West Yellowstone in July—all looking for the best fishing.

Not being a fisherperson you wouldn't know this, but it's tough to figure out how to fish a stream you've never fished before. Our task was made even tougher by the fact that we were only minutes from not just one, but too many world-famous trout streams—the Gallatin River, the Madison River, the Gibbon River, Specimen Creek, something called Bacon Rind Creek, etc., etc., etc. And on each of these streams, there's the further question about which sections are "fishing good" due to predictable and prolific hatches of the little bugs that trout crave.

So we fisherpeople spent most of Sunday, Monday and Tuesday poking around in these streams—doing a lot of driving, putting on our fishing costumes, rigging up our rods, flailing the water with various bug imitations, building group consensus, deciding to move on, de-rigging, de-costuming, driving, then re-costuming, re-rigging, and on and on. We made frequent stops at fly-fishing shops along the way to pick the brains of the local experts without paying for their advice— which means that their advice was worth roughly what we weren't paying for it. All of the fly shop guides told us, "You need a guide." And in retrospect, this was good advice, which we stupidly ignored. We are a proud bunch; we're a skilled bunch; we don't need instruction; and we're cheap. So, without guides (but with vacation money still in our wallets), we weren't catching anything and folks were getting a tad bit frustrated.

On Wednesday morning, I was up with the sun trying to work a crick out of my neck when I spied Hal skulking out of the communal dining room headed for his car with a cup of coffee and a bag of homemade cookies in his hand, long before the kitchen staff rang the bell calling everybody to breakfast. I think he was surprised to see anybody else up and moving around. So I asked him where he was going and got a shifty-eyed, less-than-informative response that sounded reasonable until I thought about it after he sped away.

As other folks sleepwalked their way to breakfast

looking for their first cups of coffee, I'd stop them and ask where Hal had run off to. Nobody knew.

Hal's wife, Mary, mumbled something about running in to Big Sky, and horseback riding, and poor phone service, and probably some other stuff that was equally unresponsive. So I forgot about it. I ate my breakfast with the group (sans Hal) and went off to another unproductive day of fishing.

Late in the day, we proud but guideless and unproductive fisherpeople returned to the ranch for dinner. We had worked hard all day. Or at least, most of us had. Just after lunch, Annie stowed her rod and waders and started walking back to our cabin saying she could catch just as many fish from the comfort of her bed and she wasn't going to miss her nap just to prove that she could tough it out streamside. We also lost Steve around 3:00pm; he left saying that his life was getting shorter by the moment, that he was going to read his book, and that he'd appreciated all he could of nature for one day.

Headed down the path that ran from our cabin porch directly to the dining hall, I remembered that Hal was still missing and sure enough when Annie and I arrived at our table, Hal's chair was still empty. This was becoming quite the little mystery—the Yellowstone version of "Where in the World is Hal?" As Mary took her seat, I was pleased to see that John and Susan were already laying for her and they were quick to pounce with a barrage of questions about Hal's disappearance.

As the questions poured down upon her, you could

see that Mary was weakening and about to break when, much to her relief, Hal walked in and headed to our table with a big grin on his face. Mary greeted him with a chorus of "I never told them a thing, honey bear. They tried, but couldn't weasel anything out of me."

"So," Paul says, "where you been, Hal?"

"Fishing," says Hal.

"Fishing where?" Susan asks.

"Down river," Hal replies.

"Down what river?" I say.

"Gallatin," Hall says.

You could tell that this was going to take a long time.

Finally John says, "C'mon Hal. Spill it. You'll not get a moment's rest until you come clean."

And that's when Hal told his story. It went something like this:

"Okay. So I got a *guide*. Big deal. Laugh all you want. But I caught fish. Lots of fish. Mostly big fish. On mostly dry flies fished within a few yards of my big feet. And I had a good time—a really good time. And learned a lot about catching big trout—all *fifty* of them—from my *guide*. "

And that brought down the house. The word "fifty" shot across that dining hall, careened off the antlers of the big moose on the wall, echoed down the hall into the kitchen and came back to our table followed by a very large crowd of campers and staff bee-lining their way toward Hal's chair.

Now, I know you're not much on fishing and proba-

bly don't really care, but catching *fifty* trout in one day (with or without a guide) when the rest of the nearby world is catching *nada* is a major feat—one worthy of intense questioning and repeated storytelling.

So Hal told his fishing story of carefully working his way down the steep river embankment to a rock ledge covered in just a couple of feet of raging Gallatin River water. He told of peering over the edge of that bankside ledge into the emerald green depths of the river, unable to see the bottom. He told of standing next to his guide, both of them surveying the water for casting targets. He told of casting his caddis fly imitation no more than 10 yards upstream, watching it wash back toward him, and the huge rainbow trout that came out of nowhere from below that ledge to take his fly and run straight across the river with it—jumping maybe 30 or 40 times (that's a lot) trying to escape Hal's clutches. He told of the eagle that swooped in from his perch in a tree high above the river and tried in vain to steal Hal's trophy. He told of gradually working that big trout back to the slower water below him, netting him and releasing him unharmed back to into the holding water at his feet.

And then he told about the next trout that he deftly coaxed to his fly . . . and on and on and on . . . story after story . . . from fish number two to fish number fifty . . . casting right-handed for a while and then left-handed . . . until he was exhausted and could fish no more . . .

We—guests and ranch staff alike—were mesmerized. Before our very eyes, Hal developed a presence that was irresistible. We sat at his feet and watched a halo form a complete circle around his head. We sought wisdom; but we all knew Hal and figured wisdom was a reach; so we sought directions . . . to the scene of his miraculous catch.

At dawn the next morning, John, John, Susan, Steve, Paul, Barbara, Annie and I piled into cars full of our gear and headed to the place we all already called "Hal's Spot." We had cajoled Hal into dictating explicit instructions, which Mary copied down for us and handed out. (I managed to get the first copy, which I got Hal to autograph. It now hangs in a frame on the wall of my office.) We figured leaving at daybreak would insure us all strategic positions along the stretch of river now known to the entire ranch community as Hal's Reach.

Well, we were too late. Somehow the word was already out. Montana State police officers had the road barricaded—stopping all motorized traffic up and down the now famous stretch of river. They tried in vain to check the surging crowd. From our cars, now stranded in backed-up traffic, we could see a flotilla of whitewater rafts that had been commandeered by fisherpeople and floated into positions all along Hal's Reach. Several hundred fishermen stood elbow to elbow casting caddis fly imitations and tripping over the rafts as they ebbed and flowed in the current. One lone fisherman stood on a huge, smooth, round granite boulder in the middle of the stream and cast beautiful, tight fly line loops to present his fly. A local standing by our car and watching the circus with us visitors informed us that the boulder was the very one made famous in *A River Runs Through It* when Brad Pitt stood atop it and tossed his fly line every which way for the camera.

A local TV news truck was parked inside the barricades and a buxom brunette outfitted in a sleeveless black silk shirt, tight-fitting white slacks and fire-engine red pumps was stumbling from officer to officer along the gravel road shoulder, seeking interviews and information on the fishing and Hal's whereabouts. Her cameraman followed behind her like a well-trained dog, pulling a load of wires and filming everything in sight.

For the next few hours, we watched the crowd build as folks—stuck miles from the scene in standstill traffic—hiked in to see what all the ruckus was about. Most carried fly rods and wore fishing vests; many also wore waders or carried them slung over their shoulders.

By noon, there were several hotdog vendors pushing their carts into position beside the barricades; a bearded guy with thick black-rimmed glasses set up his sno-cone truck a short distance up the road; a heavy-set blonde lady wandered the crowd selling an assortment of buttons, baseball caps, miniature pennants and tiny baseball bats—all carrying the familiar "Yankees" logo—from a box tethered around her neck. An older couple, wearing his and hers tie-dyed T-shirts and paisley-decorated green headbands, had opened the doors to their VW bus and were waving an "Area 51" banner while onlookers circled them, gawking at homemade posters showing photos of UFO crash sites.

Helicopters sporting call letters from radio stations as far away as Missoula circled overhead reporting on the action. Periodically a chant would erupt from the crowd, "We want Hal. We want Hal. We want Hal." John, John, Susan, Steve, Barbara, Paul, Annie and I soon became minor celebrities as word circulated that we knew Hal and could identify him. We quickly lost our following, however, when they figured out that none of us knew where Hal was.

At one point a rather large and slightly balding man wearing a Hoss Cartwright-style hat tried to penetrate the crowd but had to be whisked away to safety by local rescue squad members when someone mistakenly pointed to him and yelled, "There's Hal now." The whole place was out of control and the policemen behind the barricades called in reinforcements to help control the crowd, which according to several whispered estimates was approaching 10,000 in number.

Well, I'm guessing you can picture the rest. It took several more hours for the assembled masses to figure out that "we should all have been here yesterday" because none of the fisherpeople lining the river bank were catching anything—not even the guy on the boulder who was no longer fishing but just sitting there watching the show. There was one young guy claiming at the top of his lung capacity that he'd caught one "just down around the bend" but his claim was heavily discounted because he had no witnesses.

As reality set in, the disappointed gathering gradually dispersed. By 5:00pm the barricades were removed and traffic started to creep again. A little before 7:00pm things were loosening up enough that we managed to get our vehicles dislodged from the gridlock and pointed back toward the ranch. A little after 7:00pm, Annie and I arrived back at our cabin and hustled into fresh clothes to get to dinner before the kitchen shut down.

As we ran down the dusty path toward the dining hall, Jolie and Marshall came up to meet us and said that they'd heard we were stuck in traffic all day and were sorry about that, but wanted us to know that Hal was down having dinner with the mayor and the governor and had asked Marshall and Jolie to pass on his apologies since he wouldn't be dining with the rest of us that night. Apparently he'd said something about his tight schedule and that he was thinking about trying to fit us in for a few minutes to have coffee with him sometime "the day after tomorrow"—but not to get our hopes up. That's when Marshall pointed out a helicopter parked out in the pasture below the stables in the middle of a field full of cars and trucks and told us that, due to the traffic snarl that had shut down most of southwest Montana, it was the only way the governor and the mayor could get to the ranch.

As we approached the dining hall we could see a horde of people outside the front doors pushing and shoving for a turn at peering through the windows to get a glimpse of Hal. Linda, the ranch manager, saw us and waved for us to follow her around behind the dining hall to the staff dining room where they were serving dinner to ranch guests while Hal met with the governor and the mayor in the main dining room. She said that they'd had to clear the hall of most of its tables so the press, FBI and local police could all get in. I asked her what the FBI had to do with any of this and she told us that while Hal was inside telling his story over and over again to his adoring fans, the FBI had showed up, flashed their badges and expressed some skepticism about Hal's claims. They were now inside listening patiently to every re-telling of Hal's fishing conquest.

After Annie and I had gulped down our dinners— we'd only had a hotdog and a sno-cone to eat since dinner the night before—we found Linda and begged her to find us a way into the main dining hall so we could hear Hal's story just one more time. After some negotiating and arm-twisting, Linda found us a spot just inside the kitchen doors where we got a surprisingly good view of Hal who was seated at the head of one of the long dining tables flanked by the governor and the mayor. Hal was taking questions from the press who were being held at bay by a couple of police officers and a very large German shepherd. Apparently Hal had just finished another re-telling of his stories—fish by fish.

One of the reporters from *The New York Times* was in the middle of asking Hal about the exact length of fish #43 when he was pretty rudely interrupted by one of the FBI officers who said that he'd just tallied up all of Hal's fish stories and had come up one short. He'd only counted 49 individual fish stories when Hal had, for the past 24 hours, been saying he'd caught 50 fish.

There was sudden silence in the room. You could have heard a caddis fly drop onto the floor of that great hall. All eyes shifted to Hal—looking for Hal to set that agent straight, to show that agent how he'd miscounted, or to remember the one fish story he'd inadvertently left out of this most recent re-telling and tell it so the agent would have his 50 stories. But that's not what happened. This is what Hal said:

"Oh, yeah, I guess you're right. Now that I think about it, I did only catch 49 fish. I just said 50 because I was *rounding up*."

So, that was it . . . and that was the end of it. The silence persisted and deepened. Eyes were averted. The press started packing up their gear. The governor hustled out the door followed closely by the mayor—both appearing fearful that Hal's little indiscretion would rub off on them. As the governor made his way through the crowd outside the hall, one crowd member yelled, "Hey, Governor, what's Hal like? Did you get to shake his hand?" and the governor replied, "Hal who?"

You could hear the engines on the helicopter catch fire and rev to a high pitch. The crowd outside the hall was now full of whispers as word spread that Hal had *rounded up*. The FBI agents moved in, took Hal by the arms, and said, "I'm afraid you'll have to come with us."

Before long, Annie and I were left standing in that hall all alone with Mary, Hal's wonderful wife who, until just a couple of minutes before, had been standing beside her husband's chair listening with familial pride to her husband's incredible stories.

We tried to console her but she was having none of it. As we were heading for the door, one of the kitchen staff turned out the dining hall lights. Dark descended. And Mary stood in the middle of that hall, in the darkness, and said to nobody in particular, "How fitting. Moments ago Hal and I were a couple standing on top of the world. Fisherpeople the world over have embarked on pilgrimages to visit us. Other women envied me because I was the lucky one—the woman behind the newly famous man. Several movie studios had already contacted us about the film rights. The town of Big Sky was mounting a campaign to rename the big rock that stands in the middle of the river in honor of Hal calling it "Hal's Head." Hal was destined to have his own page in the annals of fisherdom until he . . . *rounded up*."

Two days later, the McLeod clan got up real early

and started the long drive back to Walla Walla. Unfortunately, we did not get to say goodbye to Hal who was being detained at an undisclosed location. John speculated that he may have been flown out of the country. Mary said that he was doing okay—that she's been allowed to take one phone call from Hal and he sounded okay, slightly humbled and a little contrite. Hal's lawyer had told her that he felt good about getting Hal released before we all arrived back at the ranch next year. We left somewhat encouraged, but we've heard nothing since.

So, there you go. Hal's experience was a lesson to me. I am minding my p's and q's and double-checking all my facts as I write my next book. The checking is slowing me down a bit but it's better than a long ride in an unmarked car to an undisclosed location. I'm trying hard not to exaggerate or embellish anything. I am being especially careful not to . . . *round up*. So you can rest assured that everything I'm writing you is the gospel truth—unadulterated and unadorned.

Please tell Charlie, Bernard and Lelia we say "hi," and please quit talking about coming out for a visit . . . Enough talk . . . Just come on. We'd love to see you.

Best,
SAM

Visitors from the Cosmos

Dear Timothy:

Thanks for the heads-up on the book. I'll probably get into town tomorrow sometime. I'll go by the bookstore and see if they have it.

Now, one good turn deserves another so I'll recommend that you go pick up a copy of *The Fabric of the Cosmos,* by Brian Greene. It is out in paperback and is written in something close to plain English so even a guy like me can sort of follow along.

Since we moved out here on the prairie, I am finding that one of my favorite pastimes is sitting on the porch after the sun goes down, listening to the frogs croak and the coyotes howl, and gazing up into the big sky that we have overhead. On a moonless night, the stars are spectacular. I guess that one of these days I'll go out and get myself a telescope, but for now I'm pretty content with my star chart and my own two eyes.

Some nights I can convince Annie to sit out there with me after dark but only on the exceptionally warm ones. Even in July, it's nice and cool out here after the sun goes down, although my definition of "cool" is often Annie's definition of "too cold."

Anyhow, I like looking up at that star-filled sky, musing on the things I've read in various astronomy and cosmology books. The fact that there are more than 100 billion galaxies out there beyond our own Milky Way just plain fascinates me. It makes me feel pretty small and insignificant—sitting on the porch of our little house in a small town out on the prairie, on our little planet spinning around an average sort of star, way out on the perimeter of a galaxy that is only one of an incomprehensible number of galaxies in our universe. And then there's the fact that a lot of the light I'm seeing coming in from some of those galaxies left there a couple of million years ago, so what I'm really seeing is those galaxies as they looked way back in time. Well, it's mind-boggling.

I often think about the odds of there being other life out there. I'm no cosmologist. I'm not a physicist. I'm not an astronomer. (Like I said, I don't even own a telescope.) And I'm certainly no philosopher. I'm no preacher either, but it does seem to me that we're being pretty full of ourselves if we believe that we're the only somewhat intelligent beings in the universe. I guess I've come to believe that there must be lots of different types of life out there and that, on average, some of those life forms are likely to be much brighter and more capable than we are—that we probably aren't all that special in the grand scheme of things. But whatever you believe, I've got a very short story to tell you.

A couple of weeks ago, Bryce and Marni were staying out here at the farm while we went on a week's vacation to Montana. One night, they were both out—right at dusk—putting the alpacas up for the night. The way they tell it, a large green ball roughly the size of a small house zoomed into the sky just above our little town of Lowden, hovered there for several minutes while they watched it spin, and then flew off at an unbelievable speed. That was it. It wasn't like anything they'd ever seen; it moved at a speed that they could only imagine; and they both saw the same thing.

Now, that's a weird one. And what makes it even more remarkable? I saw the same thing last night. I wouldn't describe it a bit differently. It was one of the most amazing things I've ever seen. I found myself accepting the fact that it was a spaceship and wondering what it looked like on the inside and what the visitors inside were like. I haven't shaken it yet.

And then yesterday I was telling this story to Jeffrey who said he and a bunch of other people saw the same thing years ago down south of Walla Walla—green ball and all.

I know you're sort of into this stuff and I don't mind telling you about this. But I hope you'll keep it to yourself. The folks around here do not need to start believing that I'm any stranger than I already seem to them. Many of them probably already think I was once abducted by aliens and returned to Earth exhibiting some unusual quirks. And it'd spook Annie to no end. I'd never get her back out on the porch at night and she'd be wanting me to go with her every evening when she goes out to the barn to check on her animals.

Anyway, I thought you'd be interested. Tell Dawn we say "hi," and encourage her to get her birding group out here for an "owling" night.

Best,
SAM

Annie Leaves the Gate Open (At Least, I'm Pretty Sure It Was Her)

Dear Liz:

I really liked your story about Hannah and the alpacas. That girl is thinking. All she needs now is a sugar daddy to buy her that fancy animal. She clearly inherited your expensive tastes.

Seriously, we're glad Hannah's enjoying the alpacas so much. Annie loved having her along at the big alpaca show. Annie says she was good company for the weekend.

Talking about finding Hannah a sugar daddy reminds me of Marshall when she was Hannah's age. It's amazing what kids hear and how they puzzle their way through new things. Marshall came home one day from 7th grade and found me in my home office. After the normal chatter about school and friends, Marshall put her mouth on pause for a few seconds and then said, "Hey Dad, what's a 'kept woman'?"

A little surprised, I said, "Where in the world did you hear that?"

And she said, "At school. Mr. Hardcastle was talking today in history class about a lady and said that she was a 'kept woman'. None of us knew what he was talking about."

"Well," I said. "A 'kept woman' is a lady who marries a rich husband and gets him to buy her a big house with a pool where she sunbathes all day and eats bon-bons and works on her nails with a long nail file."

Marshall then gets this real quizzical look on her face and says, "Hmm . . . that's funny. I don't get it. Mr. Hardcastle was talking about being a 'kept woman' like it was a bad thing."

I guess being a "kept woman" sounded pretty good to Marshall.

Anyway, that's not why I'm writing. As Hannah has probably told you, Annie now has ten alpacas—five males and five females. They're all in pastures down below the barn during the day and stabled in the barn at night. Annie's "boys" are kept separate from her "girls" but aside from guarding against unplanned sex, pasturing these animals is pretty straightforward. Alpacas eat a little orchard grass and drink a little water every day. And Annie feeds them some special alpaca pellets every night before they go to bed. (They love those pellets.) But other than that, there's not much to it.

Last week, a baby girl alpaca was born. She's our first newborn. We named her Prairie—a fitting name because she was born out here on the prairie and is the color (sandy brown) of the dirt and dust that seems to find its way into every nook and cranny of our house whenever we get a good blow.

Prairie's birth was a call to action for our dogs. They adore the new baby and are constantly worrying over her. Sam sleeps in the stall where Prairie and her mom stay at night, while Yoda and Annie patrol the fence lines looking for intruding coyotes. The goat, Bobo, spends most of each day playing with Prairie under the watchful eye of mom who spits at Bobo if she gets a little too rough. It has been very interesting to watch the animals take Prairie under their collective wing and help raise her. You should get Hannah to bring you out for a visit when you get a chance. Prairie is growing up fast—too fast.

Anyway, last night well after dark, I went out to turn on a sprinkler by the front porch and there, with eyes glowing in the reflected light from inside the house, stood four of Annie's male alpacas. That wouldn't be such an odd thing except that they're never in the yard. Somehow they'd escaped from their stall in the barn. Somebody had left the gate open. So, I called out to Annie to tell her that we had some escapees and yelled over to the cottage to let Jolie know we needed a little help. (She's staying here for a few weeks until she goes off to graduate school.)

Now, alpacas are about the nicest animals on the planet. They're cute in a "frou-frou" sort of way— fluffy coats of soft fleece with Lyle Lovett hairdos and long glamorous eyelashes. They're also very graceful as they bound around in the pastures playing in the early morning when Annie lets them out of the barn to graze. They don't bite or kick and only occasionally spit at each other when they get a little annoyed. Their

only real defense is a good offense—they can run like sprinters.

And that presents a problem in big open spaces. They can be good companions and some are even affectionate, but almost none of them likes to be caught. Their instinct is to flee when approached by anything bigger than a mouse, and it is a powerful instinct.

Now, I'm not the animal person in our house and, according to Annie, I'm not very good at reading body language—human or otherwise—but you could read the look in the eyes of these freedom-loving males. They were having an unplanned boys' night out and they were enjoying it.

We needed a plan to get them back in the barn and we didn't have one, so rather than stop and think before acting, we did what we're so good at doing—

acting without thinking. And that involved running around in the dark trying to coax them back into the barn, which wasn't where they wanted to be. The choice between eating more hay or nibbling on the low-hanging sunflowers that Annie has planted around the house was not what you'd have called a tough one.

I went one way around the house while Annie went the other. Jolie was still nowhere to be seen. Within seconds after running off the porch into the dark, I managed to step into one of the many holes our dogs dig in the yard every day. They're great dogs but like every living thing, they have their unattractive habits.

I heard a little popping noise coming from the vicinity of my left calf and felt a sharp pain in my left ankle. I thought about just lying there and waiting to be discovered, writhing in pain, and suffering silently through the ambulance ride to the hospital where the emergency room staff would marvel at the fact that I was still alive. But I found a little voice inside my brain saying, "What would Lance Armstrong do?" So, I was up in no time and off in a limping trot to keep those guys from running back out into the front yard.

I could hear Annie yelling for me to block the side yard gate as the "boys" turned the corner and headed right for me. Once they realized that there was no clear way around me, they turned and headed back around the house to Annie. That's when I moved up— holding my arms out wide on either side of me to present as formidable an obstacle as possible.

I could make out the outline of a tree in the moonlight, but forgot that we'd staked them to keep them from blowing away in our next valley breeze. I promptly tripped over the rope that attached the trunk of that tree to its metal stake. That's when I went down for the second time—this time on my right knee, mostly because I was already favoring my left leg and wanted to keep it from further, most likely irreparable, injury. All that good split-second thinking left me with a bad left calf and a very painful right knee—one of those head-on knee cap bangs that hurts like childbirth and keeps on hurting even as you think that the excruciating pain can't last.

Even so, I remembered my farmer's oath, struggled back to my feet and headed toward the barn—rebooting on Lance-inspired grit. There I saw all four of Annie's "boys" slip by her and head back into the front yard on her side of the house. Again, without thinking, I turned and hobbled back to the front yard to head them off and steer them back into Annie's quadrant of the yard. I yelled around the house for Annie to see if she could roust Jolie out of the cottage to help us but got no reply as she ran back toward the barn following the "boys" who'd now broken into two groups in a divide-and-confuse sort of strategy. It was clear who was winning and it wasn't the good guys.

That's when I caught my arm on the head of a nail protruding from a fence post. As far as I remember, I felt no additional pain, but I now had two bad legs and a gash on my right arm gushing torrents of my own blood.

(Annie is reading this and saying that it wasn't a gash;

it was a scratch. And it wasn't gushing torrents; the skin was hardly torn. And I say that's just semantics.)

Seeing my own blood has always caused me to feel slightly faint. In the darkness, I couldn't see the blood, but I could feel it and feeling it was enough to cause me to feel a little sick to my stomach. I wasn't sure that I could struggle on.

And that's when Jolie appeared at the barn door with a big bowl of alpaca pellets, shook it a few times and led the "boys" very easily to their stall. Annie and I stood there—speechless. Jolie's thinking and then acting turned out to be way more effective than our acting without thinking.

Well, that was enough for me. I dragged my useless legs back into the house pulling myself along with a bloodied arm. I retired to my TV chair with a box of band-aids (the big ones), one of those cold packs real athletes use to discourage swelling, and a large bag of frozen peas (because we only had one cold pack and I had two major injuries requiring ice therapy). After I stanched the bleeding, I propped both legs up on the footstool and put the cold pack under my calf and the frozen peas on my knee.

Annie showed up in the doorway to report that Jolie had gone back to bed, that she was going to bed, and then laughed uproariously. And that's when I suggested to Annie that she close the stall gate from now on—in my very nicest and most courteous tone of voice.

Best,
SAM

It's Not About the Book . . .
It's About the Cover!

Note to Reader: Ernest "Boots" Mead was a professor of mine at the University of Virginia. He taught music . . . and a lot more. He taught me the meaning of "A" and for that I am forever grateful.

Dear Boots:

I got your letter and appreciated the nice things you said about *Welcome to Walla Walla*. I sensed that you *liked* the book, but *loved* the cover. You are not the only one who *loved* the cover. The cover is doing a nice job of selling the book; so folks are judging the book by its cover. In this case, I think that's a good thing.

Since you liked the cover so much, you might like to know how it came to be. Jeffrey's artwork is all over Walla Walla—paintings on canvas, murals on the walls of local wineries and other businesses, and bronze sculptures. He's well known here locally—mostly as a painter of vineyard scenes. So, I'd seen his artwork but didn't know him. I had to go find him . . . I digress (something I'm getting good at) . . .

Jeffrey grew up here in Walla Walla. He started painting when he was in kindergarten. His dad was an amateur cartoonist and encouraged his son's drawing.

One day back in 4th grade, Jeffrey stayed in from recess to draw on the blackboard. When his teacher saw his work, she contacted the art teacher at Walla Walla High School. When he saw Jeffrey's work, he arranged for young Jeffrey to come to the high school several afternoons a week where he could tutor the boy. In 8th grade, Jeffrey's middle school principal asked him to paint several large panels depicting athletic events to be hung in the gym—his first mural.

As Jeffrey will tell you, he was very fortunate to grow up in a place that was so encouraging of his artistic talent. Folks in town were always looking for ways to support his artwork. He had great teachers . . .

Jeffrey continued painting through high school, graduated and went on to attend Whitman College here in Walla Walla where he studied Art and Art History. He experimented with subject matter, style, medium and materials. He continued to listen and learn from his teachers but he also began to develop his own way—his own sense of himself and his talent.

In 1978 he graduated from Whitman and the next year he married Kathryn. In retrospect that turns out to have been a very good move on Jeffrey's part; Kathryn has been such a good breadwinner that Jeffrey never has had to do a stint as a starving artist.

After working in Seattle for a couple of years, Jeffrey was accepted as an intern at Sotheby's where he studied fine art, decorative arts, the art of appraisal and languages. And that ten-month stay in London opened Jeffrey's eyes to the business of art.

He and Kathryn returned to the Northwest where they settled back into Seattle. Kathryn became an avionics software engineer while Jeffrey worked as an appraiser of antiques and built his own business locating and selling mission-style furniture.

Their girls, Ellyn and Janet, were born. Life got complicated with both parents working. And Seattle started to close in on them. Jeffrey yearned for the rolling hills in the valley where he grew up, where the light plays magically in the wheat fields, in the vineyards, and on the mountains. He wanted to get back to Walla Walla.

In 1996, they packed up and moved back to the old family place out in the country just south of town. The house had fallen on hard times after Jeffrey moved away and badly needed a facelift. That meant the family would live for six months in a 40-foot trailer while the place got fixed up. (Having lived in our old Airstream for a few weeks while our farmhouse got done, Annie is marveling at that one.)

Anyway, the house got cleaned up. Kathryn was able to continue her career working remotely from their new home, the girls got settled in school, and Jeffrey planted a vineyard in what had been a big alfalfa field behind the house. He grew his vines. He worked the soil, he fought the weeds and the bugs, he pruned and shaped, and helped those vines find their own way in the vibrant sunlight. The vineyard did very well.

Once everybody was resettled, Jeffrey went in search of work and found that there was significant demand here locally for "vineyard art." He started

painting local vineyard scenes and the migrant work-
ers who helped give them life—all in the light of long
summer days and cool summer evenings. He'd found
his setting and people flocked to see his work. He was
quickly dubbed the "Vineyard van Gogh" of Walla
Walla and, as I said way back at the beginning of this
letter, his artwork is all over town. Folks around here
can't get enough of it.

So, when Annie nudged me into writing *Welcome to
Walla Walla*, I went in search of somebody here locally
to do some sort of artwork for the cover. I really
hadn't thought about it much beyond that.

And that's when Lonnie said, "You should talk to
Jeffrey. He's pretty good." (By now you know that,
here in understated Walla Walla, "pretty good" is high
praise.)

Now, finding Jeffrey is not easy. He is a man of mystery. There's no art gallery with his name on it. There's
no studio with his name on it. Nobody seems to know
his phone number, or his email address. But lots of
folks know that Jeffrey will have the odd glass of wine
at Vintage Cellars. So, I went there—several days in a
row. It was tough duty. A few days into the mission—
shortly after lunch—I was sitting at the bar, minding
my own business, when Lonnie said, "There he is,
Sam. Here comes your artist."

I don't know exactly what I was expecting but I'd
pictured the Vineyard van Gogh as a gaunt figure with
long stringy hair, maybe in a ponytail, and a beard,
probably one of those pointy little goatees. And he'd
probably have a crazed look emanating mostly from

his left eye. Well, he didn't have any of those features. He was surprisingly well kempt and well mannered—sort of a disappointment.

That was my introduction to Jeffrey. We talked for a few minutes and agreed that any further conversation should take place over a plate of cheese, and some fruit, and a glass of good local cabernet.

Long story short, I handed Jeffrey a copy of the rough manuscript. He walked off with it. To his credit, he read it. To his further credit, he said he liked it. He said he had an idea. He said he'd get back to me.

Two weeks later, I got a call from Jeffrey. (I still didn't have his phone number.) He invited me out to his "studio"—the living room of his house full up with easels, canvases, paints, a boom box, and an old sofa where Dusty, the dog, hangs out with Jeffrey while he works his magic.

In those two short weeks, Jeffrey had produced 90% of the cover you see on the book. I'd delivered some photos of the local characters that were written into the book, but otherwise had had nothing to do with it. He'd read the book, developed his own images, and put them together in a masterful way. I was impressed; it was better than anything I'd envisioned for the cover.

A week later the painting was hanging on the wall in my office and we had a mock-up of the cover. The whole process was fast, easy and fun—a nice combination.

You know, I've always marveled at how nicely the book came together. At every new turn along the way, the right person would mysteriously appear, join the team, and help move the book forward. Candace helped with editing, Jeffrey did the artwork, Kathy did the digital photography, John designed the cover and arranged the printing, and Tom did the final formatting. (I mostly just got in the way.)

And one more thing: All those folks work within a few blocks of one another right on Main Street here in Walla Walla. Who'd have thought?

Over the next few weeks, Jeffrey completed the line drawings and we sprinkled them throughout the book while others finished the editing and formatting . . . The book was printed . . . Boxes arrived . . . We had a small party for all those who'd helped with the book . . . And then Jeffrey and I started talking about the artwork for the next book. . .

You, of all people will understand this: Jeffrey has his own special talent and was lucky to have great teachers who helped him see it and develop it . . .

Just as I was . . . Many thanks.

Best,
SAM

The End

D ear Reader:

I hate to end this. I've enjoyed writing these letters and hope you've enjoyed reading them. If you've gotten this far, maybe you did.

Folks often ask me what I've learned from writing books. When I launch in on gathering information for a story, being disciplined about writing, and all the stuff you have to do to turn a manuscript into a book that's on a shelf where somebody can buy it, a few folks will interrupt my rambling and say, "I want to know what you've learned from *writing*—not all that other stuff." Hmmm . . . it's an interesting question.

Questions like this require a thoughtful response and a thoughtful response requires some musing on the subject . . . Oh no, here is Annie again—looking over my shoulder. She is telling me that there is already too much musing in this book and that I should give it a rest. She wants to go for a walk down by the river; so she says I should go easy on you readers and keep it short . . . Okay, I'll try.

One of the things I've learned from writing is that

there are a lot of stories out there. I keep thinking I'll run out of interesting things to write about, but every time that thought resurfaces in my brain, I meet somebody or read something or see something that reminds me how much interesting stuff is going on all the time if I'll just slow down and take notice of it. It is a good lesson and, unfortunately, it's one I have to learn over and over almost every day. (You'd think a guy'd catch on after a few days.)

Another thing I've learned: Sometimes it just isn't there—creativity, I mean. And as you can tell from reading these letters, I could use more of it—creativity, I mean.

I try to spend a couple or three hours writing every day. Some days, it's effortless. I sit down, turn on the computer, limber up my two typing fingers (I'm not a very good typist), and the words just pour out of my brain faster than my two fingers can get them down. I don't know where the words come from. When it happens, it's a wondrous thing—creativity, I mean.

But other days, I might as well be drumming my fingers on the tabletop; it'd be just as productive. On the unproductive days, I have to make myself get up from the computer and go do some of the book publishing work I don't really care for. So, maybe the universe conspires to stick in unproductive days so something will actually get published—not just written. I don't pretend to know. I do know that some days the mojo just isn't.

Now, here's Annie again saying that the phrase "slow as molasses" is not adequate to describe how painfully slow I'm being about ending this book. So, good for you, Annie, you just reminded me of another thing I've learned. (Annie is now slumped down in her easy chair moaning like she's wounded.)

Anyway, the other thing I've learned is that writing is addictive. I hate to stop. After three hours on a good writing day, I feel like I've just taken a drug-induced trip inside my head to some really good place. I feel content. I feel alive. The only potentially negative side effect is the bad humor Annie's going to lay on me if I don't get up from here and go for that walk. She thinks she knows where there's a den of coyote pups we need to go see . . . from a distance.

Until next time . . .

Best,
SAM

Sam McLeod

Photo by John Gordon

Sam McLeod was born in Nashville, Tennessee in 1951, grew up there, attended college and graduate school at The University of Virginia and Washington & Lee University, worked as a banker, a lawyer, and venture capital investor, and retired to Walla Walla, Washington with his wife, Annie, in 2004. Sam has written two books—*Welcome to Walla Walla* and this book, *Bottled Walla*. He says he wants to write some more. We'll see. . .

For more information on Sam McLeod, his books, Detour Farm, and other stuff, log on to:
www.lettersfromwallawalla.com